Fortune Favours Miss Gold

Fortune of Fates Series

Nadine Millard

This is a work of fiction. The names, characters, places, and events are either products of the author's imagination or are used fictitiously, and any resemblance to actual persons, living or deceased, business establishments, events, locales is entirely coincidental.

Copyright © 2019 by Nadine Millard
Print Edition

All rights reserved. Without limiting the rights under copyright reserved above, no part of this publication may be reproduced, stored in or introduced into a retrieval system, or transmitted, in any form, or by any means (electronic, mechanical, photocopying, recording, or otherwise) without the prior written permission of the copyright owner of this book.

To my daughter Kacy, my own golden girl!
Thank you for the inspiration and for being you.

Prologue

"Hush, Pippa. Papa will hear."

Eleanor Gold stood at the top of the sweeping staircase of her father's Grosvenor Square home.

As was his wont, their father had stumbled in the door at close to four o' clock in the morning.

Eleanor could practically smell the stench of stale alcohol and sweat even from the distance.

Beside her, her younger siblings Phillipa and Trevor trembled with fright.

It was at times like these Eleanor truly felt as though she hated her father.

She was more than used to his escapades by now, having witnessed them since she was in short skirts. But now? Now that she was the grand old age of fifteen and felt solely responsible for ten-year-old Pippa and six-year-old Trevor, her anger burnt hotter than ever before.

Why had they been saddled with such a man for their sire? Why was their mother so useless when it came to dealing with her husband, or protecting her children from his rages, his drinking, his gambling?

It was the outside of enough.

"Lost the damned thing, didn't I?"

Eleanor's ears pricked up, and a snake of dread slithered down her spine.

"Lost it?" That was her mother. Her quiet, biddable, church-mouse mother. "What do you mean you've lost it?"

"This. The house. We need to pack up and remove to Somerset."

"For heaven's sake, Augustus. What *are* you talking about?"

"Dammit, woman. Do not question me."

Eleanor winced as her father's bellows shook the rafters. Beside her, Pippa and Trevor clamped hands over their ears. She pulled them both closer, as though she could shield them from the ugliness that surrounded them every time their father had a drink.

"But, Augustus, we need a house in London if the girls are to have a proper Come Out. And what of Trevor?"

"I can win it back," the drunken lout slurred. "I just need to figure out a way. That – that young pup thinks he can ruin me?"

"Who?" her mother demanded.

This was the most Mrs. Gold had ever stood up to her husband. And it should have made Eleanor proud, but all it did was increase her fear. If things were bad enough that her mother would actually argue with her husband, then they certainly were in a world of trouble.

"Tristan Bloody Grayson," her father spat the name as though it were the blackest of curses.

"Lady Devon's boy?" Mrs. Gold gasped. "Augustus, he is but a child. How could you have lost our house to him?"

"I'll win it back, I said," her father sneered. "Didn't I tell you I would win it back? I just need some more funds."

As soon as I'm old enough, Eleanor vowed as they listened to Augustus Gold staggering around downstairs, her mother following and barking questions at him, *I'm finding a husband and getting away from him. I'll take Pippa and Trevor and make sure they never have to witness this again.*

There was a series of crashes, followed by a curse or two, and then – silence.

"He's fallen asleep," Pippa whispered.

"No doubt," Eleanor answered, unable to keep the bitterness from her young voice. "Right, the both of you to bed."

"But I don't want –"

"I don't like to sleep alone –"

"I'm scared to be by myself –"

Eleanor sighed as her siblings begged and pleaded to sleep with her as they always did when their father awoke them in the night.

"Fine, come along then," she said, sounding for all the world like a woman thrice her age.

Before long she had them settled, one on either side of her.

"Ellie?"

"Hmm?"

The night was finally still, and already Eleanor could hear the steady breathing of Trevor beside her.

"Thank you for taking care of us," Pippa whispered into the night.

Eleanor blinked back the sudden tears that formed in her green eyes.

"I'll always take care of you, Pip," she whispered back, ruffling the golden blonde curls so like her own.

"Promise?"

Eleanor gazed unseeingly into the gloom, thinking of how she could happily throttle both her father and mother when she heard such fear and uncertainty in her younger sister's tone.

"I promise."

Chapter One

Ten Years Later

"IT CAN'T ALL be gone, Mr. Smith."

Eleanor Gold sat with her hands clasped primly in her lap, her back straight against the rickety wooden chair, her face the picture of ladylike calm and decorum.

Inside she was screaming.

"I'm afraid it is, Miss Gold." The gentleman peered over his spectacles to fix her with a sympathetic yet stern stare. "Quite gone."

"But – but the house—" She struggled to keep her tone even. "There was no mortgage on the house. You said so yourself."

"So I did," the man answered calmly. He studied her for a moment or two before suddenly removing his spectacles and pinching the bridge of his nose.

"If I may speak plainly?" he asked.

Eleanor nodded and waited.

"Your father's gambling was profligate, to say the least."

Didn't she know it? Their father had gambled away

the house in Grosvenor Square, along with a hunting lodge in Scotland. It was only by the grace of God that they'd managed to hang on to the manor house in Somerset.

It had cost what little money they had left to get Eleanor and her siblings to Bath to meet with Mr. Smith.

When a missive had arrived at the house to say they had only weeks to vacate before the new owner took possession, Eleanor had felt a fear unlike anything she'd ever experienced course through her veins.

It had been near impossible to keep her worries from Pippa and Trevor, but she'd done her best.

"It must be a mistake," she had assured them. *"We shall go to see the solicitor and have the whole thing straightened out right away."*

But as she gazed across the disorderly desk of her father's solicitor, the last of Eleanor's hope died in her chest.

"Your father's debts were significant. He –" The older man paused and cleared his throat, clearly uncomfortable with the news he was about to impart. "He gambled away the Somerset house before his passing."

"No!" The gasp escaped Eleanor before she could rein it in, and a memory flashed before her eyes. She and her siblings huddled on the stairs as her father confessed he'd gambled away their townhouse.

"But – but he died five years ago, Mr. Smith. Why is this coming to light now?"

"The – ah – gentleman to whom he lost the property has been on the continent these five years past," Mr. Smith explained. "Now he is returned and, well, he wants it."

Eleanor felt a bout of tears spring to her eyes, but she would be damned if she let them fall.

Her cheeks heated with shame as she leaned forward in her chair, her hands gripping the green velvet of her travelling cloak.

"I, *we,* that is – my siblings and I –" she began to explain haltingly, spitting the words passed the lump of embarrassment lodged in her throat. "We have nothing else, Mr. Smith. We shall be quite ruined. We – we have nowhere to go."

Already, they were ruined.

At five and twenty, Eleanor was a confirmed spinster. By the time she had been old enough for a Come Out and a Season, her father's pockets had been to let.

There simply hadn't been the money to spend on a full household of servants, let alone letting a house in London and incurring the costs of a Season. And if there was no money for Eleanor, there was certainly none for Phillipa.

Trevor hadn't even been able to go to school as he should have. He was the first Gold in generations who hadn't attended Eton.

No, the children's education, after they'd lost their governess, had fallen to Eleanor.

Five years ago, upon her father's death, Eleanor had finally gotten her hands on the family ledgers to see the extent of the damage her father had done. She had always had a head for numbers.

It had made for stark reading, to be sure. But, and of this she was quite certain, there had been *no* mention of the house in Somerset being gambled away.

Oh, but the deeds. She remembered thinking it odd they weren't with the other papers.

Dread formed like a rock and settled in her stomach, for she knew it was true.

The deeds weren't there because they'd been tossed on a table and handed over to another debauched, gambling drunkard. Just as easily as her father had tossed away any and all hope of a future for his children.

"That's not necessarily true," Mr. Smith interrupted her ever-morose thoughts.

Eleanor's head snapped up and she watched as Mr. Smith dug out a folded sheaf of papers, aging and curling at the sides, and handed them over.

She opened them with shaking fingers, running her eyes quickly over the contents.

"I don't understand."

"Before your mother passed away, she came to see me."

Mr. Gold had followed his wife to the grave not two years after her demise. Eleanor and her siblings had mourned their mother a lot more than their father.

"She was never strong enough to stand up to him, I know. But she *was* clever."

Eleanor felt a surge of grief at the lawyer's words. Yes, her mother had been clever and loving. And wasted on a man such as her father.

"As I was saying, she came to see me only months before she died."

Eleanor could only gape in shock. Her mother had been sickening for years before she finally passed away, frail and wasting. It had been horrific feeling so helpless, just watching it happen.

Surely she could not have made a trip to visit a lawyer in that state?

And then Eleanor remembered. Mrs. Gold had announced that the family surgeon had recommended a fortnight in Bath, taking the healing waters.

Eleanor had offered to accompany her, but she'd been quite adamant that she would go alone, with only her devoted servant Mary for company.

When Mrs. Gold had returned, she hadn't looked any better. In fact, she'd looked worse, though it did seem as though she had found some measure of peace on her visit. She died not long after.

"You are holding the deeds to a cottage by the sea on the edge of Torrell. Your mother purchased the property with funds that she had been saving for some years," Mr. Smith explained gently. "It was not part of your father's holdings."

Eleanor could only stare. The edge of their village? And she'd never known of it!

"She gave very strict instructions that it was to be kept secret from her husband, even from her children. Her wishes were that it be passed on to you, Miss Gold, should the need arise. If and when all of her children were settled and comfortable with homes of their own, or indeed if they were to remain at the manor house, however, I was to donate it to a foundling hospital at which she volunteered."

Those dratted tears threatened again, and Eleanor blinked furiously to hold them back.

Her mother. Her poor, darling, weak mother had been incredibly strong after all.

She had saved her children in ways their father never would or could.

"I do not know the condition of the property, Miss Gold. It has been some years, as you know, since it was purchased."

"I understand." Eleanor nodded. But something was better than nothing.

"The new owner of – of the manor house," Mr. Smith continued, his tone tinged with regret. "He will be arriving in Bath within the week and, I am informed, straight on to Torrell after that. The property must be vacant for his arrival."

Eleanor could see how it pained Mr. Smith to inform her of such things.

But her heart was lighter than it had been before.

Though she still loathed the cad who had stolen her family home from her, who had left her siblings without their childhood house, at least now they had somewhere to go.

Eleanor stood and held out a hand to the aging solicitor.

He stood and clasped her hand.

"Thank you, Mr. Smith," she said, proud that her voice remained steady. "I shall ensure that the house is emptied for the gentleman's arrival."

At least whoever it was planned to retain the skeletal staff Eleanor had managed to hang on to. She would have felt a hundred times worse had her servants lost their home and livelihoods, too.

"If I may say, Miss Gold, you are a young woman of great strength and courage. You would have done very well in London."

Eleanor blinked in surprise at the unexpected compliment.

London.

She supposed that he meant she would have gone up there and batted her lashes at some wealthy gentleman or other and secured a future for herself and her siblings.

But she had been needed here. Even if they'd had the funds to allow Eleanor to be presented, she couldn't have left her siblings.

She turned to leave the small office, determined to make sure her family was nowhere near the manor house when the great big lout came to claim it.

"Mr. Smith—" A thought struck Eleanor, and she turned her head to address the solicitor.

"Miss?"

"Might I have the name of the new owner?"

Mr. Smith hesitated only a moment.

"I suppose it makes little difference now," he mumbled before nodding slightly. "A Mr. Grayson, Miss Gold. Tristan Grayson. Son of Viscount Devon."

Eleanor's blood ran ice-cold at the name.

Tristan Bloody Grayson. Her father's voice echoed in her reeling mind. The night he had been railing against the young pup to whom he'd lost their London house.

The stone of dread that had been a fixture in her stomach since the start of this meeting turned to ice as her cold anger poured into her very bones.

Tristan Grayson. She'd never met the man, yet he had been the ruination of her life since she'd been but a girl.

And still now, all these years later, he was nothing but a torment.

Chapter Two

"YOU SEE? IT is not as bad as all that," Eleanor said to Pippa, hearing the brittleness in her tone as she surveyed the cottage through the dusty carriage window.

She and Trevor had done their best over the last few days to make the cottage inhabitable, but Pippa hadn't come with them. She was afraid of spiders and mice, and Eleanor thought that would make her more a hindrance than a help.

When she had told her siblings of the change in their circumstances, their reactions had been just as she anticipated they would be.

Trevor's face had grown red, and he'd ranted and raved almost all the way back to Torrell. Even their stop at an inn along the way had been peppered with his black oaths against their mystery tormentor and all the ways he'd like to exact his revenge.

Trevor was young and hot-headed. He would learn, as Eleanor had, that there was little point in railing against Mr. Grayson. It was done. And whereas Trevor's anger was white hot and burning, Eleanor's was icy and quiet.

Trevor wished for revenge, while Eleanor merely wished the man to perdition.

Pippa, on the other hand, had wept. And wept. And wept.

She loved her sister dearly, but Pippa had a lot of their mother's docility and fragility in her. That made her sweet and loving but also little use in a crisis, unfortunately.

Still, Eleanor had rallied their spirits as best as she could and had set them to work as soon as they arrived back at the manor.

After sitting down with the staff and explaining that they would be leaving, but the house was to be kept open and running for the arrival of the new owner, Eleanor had thrown herself into packing, lest she have a moment to reflect on their circumstances and therefore fall apart.

There simply wasn't the time.

She would rather carry their belongings on her back than still be in residence when Mr. Grayson arrived.

The servants had been sympathetic and so kind that Eleanor had very nearly lost control of her emotions. But then she would remember that this man had driven them out of every house they'd ever owned, and her seething anger would fuel her to tamp down her emotions and get on with the job at hand.

It had taken but a few days to pack up their pitiful belongings.

Eleanor had sold everything of value in the house. Everything.

Mother's jewellery, the silverware, paintings, and even parts of the furniture that could fetch a price.

Their horses had been sold off as well as their carriages.

The last of them had just been sold to the local squire, who had kindly allowed them to use it to remove to their new home.

The driver would take the carriage and its team to the squire after they'd emptied it of themselves and their trunks, and that would be that.

All that remained in their possession were a set of greys who had seen better days and a rickety gig that probably wouldn't last much longer in any case.

On the morning before Mr. Grayson was due to arrive, they climbed into the carriage, squeezed in beside their trunks. Mary, who would be the only servant to accompany them, sat up top with the driver.

Eleanor didn't really have the money to retain Mary, but the woman was loyal to a fault.

"I promised your mother I would take care of you," she had told a tearful Eleanor when she'd been helping her arrange to sell off almost everything they owned just to stay afloat. "And I will keep that promise, Miss. We'll get by just fine."

They hadn't much money left, that was the crux of it.

Eleanor had bought some animals and invested in a good vegetable garden so they could at least sustain themselves.

Now though, the time had come, as she had known it would, to think about them all finding work.

How the mighty had fallen. The Gold name had always been synonymous with wealth and the upper classes.

Now that Pippa was twenty and Trevor almost a man, it was only a matter of time before they would have to scatter and find work just to survive.

Eleanor could, perhaps, stay in Torrell teaching or – or something.

Pippa might leave to become a governess. Eleanor had taught her well enough to be able to do that.

Lord knew what Trevor might be able to do. Study the law, perhaps, if they could get him a position somewhere.

She might write to Mr. Smith and see if the man needed an apprentice or knew of anyone who did.

These thoughts and worries were a constant thrumming through Eleanor's mind. Had been for years. But never more so than now.

Well, at least a cottage would be vastly cheaper to run than the manor house.

And there was room for a vegetable patch. She

could plant what she had brought from the manor house and start again.

Trevor had already penned off an area for the animals, and there was a small outhouse that could be used as a stable for the greys.

All in all, things could be much worse.

A quick glance at her siblings was enough to show they clearly did not share the sentiment.

Trevor looked angry, as usual. And Pippa's blue eyes were filling with tears. As usual.

Eleanor stifled a sigh of frustration.

"Come along then," she said as the carriage door opened and the driver helped her down from the conveyance.

Mary and the driver were already carrying trunks and valises up the small garden path to the cottage's bright red door.

Tide Cottage. Their new home. And one that at least belonged to them forever.

It was beautiful. There was no denying that.

The cottage stood on its own just off the dusty road. The garden at the front was small but would be lovely when maintained correctly. At the moment, it was quite overgrown.

The building itself looked like something from a child's storybook. Squat and made from stone of grey, it was covered in ivy that was blooming spectacularly in the warm summer sun.

Round the back, Eleanor knew since she'd been here all week cleaning and readying the place, was a much larger garden that now held the animals and the beginnings of her vegetable garden.

More than that, there was a spectacular view of the sweeping coastline. A rather stubborn gate led to a shell and rock path right to the sea.

They could bathe in the summer months and take long, brisk walks in the winter.

Truly, they were fortunate indeed to live in such close proximity to Somerset's famous beaches.

And she reminded her siblings of this fact every chance she got.

She turned and coaxed Pippa out of the carriage whilst instructing Trevor to go and help with the heavy lifting.

"It's all right, Pippa." She patted her younger sister reassuringly on the arm. "Now, there are beds to make and rooms to air. And we must start thinking about dinner." She kept her tone bright whilst she chivvied her sister up the path. "Cook packed enough hampers to last us the entire summer," she prattled on as they reached the tiny, flag-stoned entry way. "We certainly shan't starve."

Not yet, she added to herself.

She wouldn't allow such thoughts to enter her head this day. This was to be their home, and Eleanor would make it a happy one if it killed her.

TRISTAN GRAYSON RAN a discerning eye over the sizeable manor house in front of him as he drew his mount to a halt.

He didn't know what he had expected to feel as he eyed the bright, white façade that glinted in the summer sun.

Elation? Even satisfaction of some sort?

But he felt – nothing. The same nothing he'd felt when he'd obtained Gold's hunting lodge in Scotland seven years ago.

The only time he'd ever felt even a sliver of happiness in his dealings with that man had been ten years ago. The first time he'd gambled against him. The first time he'd won.

Gold had been reckless with his spending, just as Tristan's father had been. And the more he'd lost, the more irate he'd become. The more careless.

Tristan had stopped playing that night all those years ago, the second he'd won Gold's townhouse.

That was the difference between Tristan and men like his father and Mr. Gold. He knew when to stop.

He hadn't gambled for fun back then but to try to recoup some of his father's losses. Losses he'd suffered predominantly at the hands of Augustus Gold. Losses that had led him to have a massive heart attack and almost shuffle off the mortal coil, leaving a mess for his then twenty-year-old son to clean up.

That had been before Gold's fortunes began to turn, as they inevitably did with wastrels like him.

The more he lost, the more he bet. Just like the viscount.

Tristan dismounted and walked slowly up the steps toward the small staff that waited to greet him.

He eyed their expressions.

The butler was emotionless and ramrod straight, as butlers were wont to be.

But the stout lady by his side bedecked in a pristine white apron, along with the handful of maids and footmen that made up the rest of the party, couldn't quite keep the hostility from their gazes, even as they bowed and curtsied deferentially.

Well, what did he expect? Wasn't he the big, bad man who had run Gold's children from their home?

A pang of guilt tried to make itself known, but Tristan pushed it ruthlessly aside.

From the information he had on the family, he knew the daughters were twenty and twenty-five by now. He had given them plenty of time to marry and move on. The youngest Gold would be, what? Sixteen by now. So, still under the care of one of his sisters but taken care of nonetheless.

He had only wanted them to vacate when he returned from India, where he had spent the past five years working and investing to fill the family coffers again.

When he returned, he had found out, too late as it were, that the Gold children were unmarried and still occupying the manor house.

Unmarried at twenty, and especially twenty-five, most likely meant he was dealing with the plain, odd, bookish sort of spinster that was happy to remain alone. Probably bluestockings to boot.

By the time he'd arrived at the solicitor's in Bath who had been taking care of the matter, it had been too late to undo the eviction, since the family had already removed themselves to a property that had belonged to their late mother.

Tristan found himself glad that they had something their father hadn't been able to take from them. Nobody knew more than he the pain of watching your security be chipped away by a man too selfish to worry about anyone or anything outside of himself.

So, he would do his duty. Pay a call. Extend his sympathies. Express his regret that he'd unknowingly evicted them from their home. Then he would sell this property as he had Gold's others.

Perhaps then, perhaps when he got rid of the man's main residence, he would find that elusive satisfaction he craved. Satisfaction for taking everything from the man who had practically taken his father's life.

After all, the viscount was more dead than alive.

The heart attack had quickly brought on a stroke. And now he couldn't walk. Couldn't speak. He was a shell of a man. He might as well have been dead.

And the viscountess suffered daily because of it.

His father's sickness meant that the running of the viscountcy fell to Tristan.

Even at twenty, Tristan had been somewhat of a financial whizz, and he'd used that savvy to play cards just as his father had done. He'd won his first hand of cards and recouped some of the viscount's losses on the day of his twentieth birthday, and he'd been winning ever since.

The only reason Lord Devon wasn't wasting away in debtors' prison was because his son had a head for cards and business. And used it for good, rather than to play fast and loose with the family's future.

Tristan had returned from India victorious. The coffers were plentiful. The investments he'd made sound and yielding a fortune.

And this pile of bricks right here was the last thing that had belonged to Augustus Gold, the last thing that Tristan had managed to snatch from the man who had destroyed his father.

The viscount and viscountess now lived off monies that were controlled by Tristan and allowed them to maintain their lifestyle and precious reputation amongst the *ton*.

He would stay long enough in Torrell to see to the

sale of the property, extend the briefest of apologies to Gold's children for the inconvenience, and then he'd get the hell out of here.

Chapter Three

"Ellie! Ellie!"

Eleanor looked up from where she'd been tending to her vegetable garden and shielded her eyes from the bright summer sun.

Pippa came rushing toward her, waving something in her hand, and looking more animated than Eleanor had seen her in an age.

"Good heavens, what is it?" she asked as she jumped to her feet and brushed the dirt from her skirts.

The wide straw bonnet she wore protected her head from the sun, but it did nothing about the heat, and Eleanor turned her face to the ever-present sea breeze.

Dire circumstances aside, Tide Cottage really was a wonderful place to live.

She couldn't, however, push their circumstances aside forever.

Last night when Mary, Trevor, and Pippa had gone to bed, Eleanor had poured over her accounts once more.

The money she had garnered from the sale of their things had dwindled more rapidly than she was comfortable with.

It would barely see them through the winter. Their move to the cottage had accumulated costs of itself, what with making the outhouse suitable to stable the horses and make it suitable for the cow and chickens in the winter months.

It was sure to be cooler, too, this close to the sea.

Eleanor had been wracking her brain trying to think of a way to make money, but she was coming up short.

How could she break it to Pippa and Trevor, who were just becoming used to living in their new, cramped quarters?

Pippa was upon her now, so Eleanor pasted a smile on her face.

"There are *fortune tellers* in town," Pippa cried, waving a flyer under Eleanor's nose. "Can you believe it? How wonderful! We must pay them a visit."

Eleanor rolled her eyes at her fanciful sister's excitement.

"That's it?" she asked. "Fortune tellers?"

"Can you *believe* it?" Pippa demanded again.

"No, I can't." Eleanor took the paper from Pippa's hand and ran a sceptical eye over the contents. "I can't believe that anyone is foolish enough to think this claptrap is real," she finished.

"What?" Pippa frowned. "Didn't you read it?"

Eleanor looked down once again.

Come, unlock the secrets of your future and the mysteries of your past.

Learn about love, wealth, success, and more.

Have your palm read by the renowned Madame Zeta and watch all your dreams come true.

Of all the non-sensical drivel.

Eleanor sighed and shoved the flyer back into her sister's willing hands.

"Pippa, it's silly. People cannot read palms, and they most certainly cannot tell the future. Don't waste your coin on such tosh."

"Eleanor, please. When was the last time we did something frivolous? Something fun? Besides, you don't *know* that it's not real."

Eleanor glared at her younger sister as she looked imploring at her. They were of a similar height, though Pippa was slightly plumper.

Pippa also had big, blue eyes similar to Trevor's.

Eleanor's eyes had been something of an anomaly. A pale, piercing green unlike anyone else in her family.

If she hadn't looked so much like Pippa and Trevor in other ways, she would have worried about where she'd come from!

Her father had always said her eyes reminded him of a cat. And Eleanor didn't think he'd meant it as a compliment.

But that was neither here nor there. Pippa could

use her baby blues to give an imploring stare like nobody else.

It would not, however, work on her older sister who knew that every guinea was precious and shouldn't be squandered on fake fortune-tellers and tricksters.

"Pippa, we cannot –"

She was interrupted by the sound of pounding hooves approaching.

Both ladies looked up at the sound to see a man approaching on a magnificent looking horse.

Eleanor felt her breath catch in her throat as she eyed the approaching stranger.

She couldn't see much of him, squinting as she was in the bright sunlight, but she could tell he was tall. And broad shouldered.

The oddest sensation swept through her as he drew closer to the cottage and slowed to a walk. She felt as though a slow, burning heat were starting to flow through her veins.

"Who is that?" Pippa whispered.

"I have no idea," Eleanor managed past a sudden, inexplicable lump in her throat. "I'll go round the front and see."

"Ellie!" Pippa's hissed whisper brought her to a stop. "You can't go like that."

"Why?" Eleanor demanded, feeling suddenly affronted.

"Look at you!" Pippa hissed again.

Eleanor looked down and saw to her dismay that she was still wearing her gardening apron, and it was covered in dirt from the ground.

She began to quickly strip it from her, whilst Pippa tugged at her bonnet.

"Take this hideous thing off your head," Pippa demanded.

"Don't, Pippa. I –"

It was too late. Pippa had untied the ribbon and plucked her hat from her head before Eleanor could stop her.

She hadn't had a chance to put her hair up that morning. Well, she hadn't really seen the point since they didn't exactly get callers at their tiny cottage.

Her long, golden locks tumbled down her back just as a voice sounded behind them.

"I beg your pardon, I'm looking for Miss Gold."

Pippa's eyes widened then darted to Eleanor's.

For her own part, Eleanor fixed her sister with a beady glare that promised retribution, before she pulled back her shoulders and turned to face their unexpected visitor.

And gasped aloud.

She couldn't help it.

Standing before her was the single most handsome man she had ever seen.

Her eyes raked greedily over him of their own volition.

He towered above her, making her feel positively diminutive. The shoulders were just as broad as she'd garnered when he'd been some distance away. She could see that his arms were strong and his stomach flat, encased as they were in a deep green superfine.

And never had she seen fawn breeches and shiny black hessians look so mouth-watering.

Her eyes travelled back to his face, and she saw with no small amount of mortification that he was staring at her, staring at him.

Her cheeks scalded, even as her eyes continued to appreciate the strong jawline, the chestnut locks that fell across his brow, the piercing blue eyes, the supremely kissable lips…

"Eleanor." Her sister spoke and for one wild second, Eleanor was afraid she'd listed the man's attributes aloud.

Her cheeks grew hotter still as she realised that not only had she been practically drooling over this tall stranger, but she was standing there with her hair falling around her shoulders like some sort of lightskirt.

"Yes, what? Yes," she stammered, her mortification growing by the second.

Taking a steadying breath, she schooled her features to polite indifference as though they were meeting in a ballroom and not in her cabbage patch.

"I am Miss Gold," she said, grateful that her voice was steady.

"So am I," Pippa piped up, and Eleanor turned to scowl at her before facing the stranger once more.

"I am Miss Eleanor Gold," she clarified. "This is my younger sister, Miss Phillipa Gold. How may we help you?"

The stranger continued to stare for a moment longer before he shook his head slightly as though awakening from some sort of trance.

"Miss Gold." His deep baritone ran along her nerve endings, and Eleanor shivered in the heat of the summer's day.

Good heavens. How ridiculous.

He stopped speaking again, and Eleanor frowned in confusion.

She threw a quick glance at Pippa, but she looked just as baffled.

"Er – yes?" she prompted.

"Sorry, I –" He stopped again, and Eleanor wondered if he was a bit daft in the head.

The stranger smiled suddenly, his wry, crooked grin causing her stomach to flip.

"I wasn't expecting – well, you," he said softly.

"Well, we weren't expecting you, either, Mr.—?" she asked, trying to ignore how the sea breeze played with his hair, clenching her fists so she wouldn't act on the mad urge to follow suit.

She watched as he took a deep breath then fixed a charming smile on her. One that no doubt charmed more than one lady out of her virtue.

Pippa sighed beside her, and Eleanor stiffened at the sound. It would be just like Pippa to imagine herself in love with a handsome stranger who had barely spoken three words to her.

Just like Pippa. Not Eleanor. Most definitely not like Eleanor.

"My name is Mr. Grayson," he said, and Eleanor froze in shock. "Mr. Tristan Grayson. And I –"

She didn't give him a chance to finish. What was there to say, in any case? That cold, icy anger that had been carrying her through the last couple of weeks suddenly exploded and grew hotter than the sun.

"How dare you?" she hissed and watched with some small amount of satisfaction as his eyes widened, and he actually stepped back a bit.

Without another word, she took hold of Pippa and dragged the younger lady toward the cottage.

"Miss Gold, please. I want to explain."

She could hear that he hurried after them, and she would be damned if she let him take one step inside this home. He had taken all of her others. He wouldn't take even a mouthful of the *oxygen* in this one.

"Go inside the house," she told Pippa, and it was a testament to how angry she must look that Pippa nodded, wide-eyed, then dashed inside.

"Explain *what?*" Eleanor demanded as she wheeled around to face him. "Explain how you took everything from us? How you ruined our lives as children and have continued to ruin them right up until now? How you took from us the only home we've ever known? How you destroyed us and any chance of a future?"

She would regret this outburst, Eleanor knew. In some small, still sane part of her brain, she knew that she would be thoroughly ashamed when her white hot anger had burnt out.

But for now, for now she wanted to rail against him, to throw the weapons of her words at him and hope they made some sort of mark.

"You are a selfish, gambling, *cad* just like my father was!" She was breathless in her fury. Burning with rage.

"Well, you can have the house in London and the manor house. You can have your blasted hunting lodge and everything else you took from us. But you cannot have this cottage, and you *cannot* have another second of my time. Get off my property and don't come back."

She spun on her heel and dashed inside, slamming the door with a satisfying bang.

Pippa was standing in the entry way, eyes almost popping from her head.

"You were magnificent, Ellie," she breathed.

But Eleanor didn't feel magnificent. She felt angry and humiliated and filled with impotent, anxious energy.

"Get your cloak," she suddenly bit out, and Pippa jumped at her tone.

Taking a steadying breath, Eleanor worked at calming herself so she wouldn't bite her poor sister's head off.

"Wh-where are we going?" Pippa asked hesitantly.

Eleanor needed to get out of here. She needed to walk off her temper. She needed a distraction from the fact that the person responsible for her ruin, and the ruin of her siblings, was also the most beautiful thing she'd ever seen.

Suddenly, she just wanted to be young and frivolous and forget that she had the weight of the world on her shoulders. Just for today. Just for a moment.

"Let's go and get our fortunes told," she managed, smiling as Pippa squealed her excitement and dashed off.

Perhaps the frivolity of fortune telling was just what she needed to take her mind off the infuriating man who had ruined her life.

Chapter Four

WELL, THAT COULD have gone better.

Tristan staggered back to his horse, his mind spinning from the short and altogether unpleasant encounter with Miss Gold.

Good God, he hadn't been prepared for *her*.

When he'd decided that he would call on the Gold family, after he'd been served an almost inedible meal that he was fairly sure the cook had burnt on purpose, he had thought he would be meeting with well, a spinster.

Miss Eleanor Gold.

She might be older than any other single lady of his acquaintance, but she was no spinster. Certainly not the type he would have expected.

When he'd rounded the corner, following the sound of voices, he hadn't been sure what to expect.

It certainly hadn't been the sight of two young ladies grappling over some sort of bonnet.

As he'd watched, the smaller one had pulled the contentious object off the head of the other, and Tristan had felt his breath hitch as he'd watched a waterfall of golden curls tumble around the lady's slender shoulders and down her back.

His throat had grown drier than the sands of the Indian desert, and he'd found himself wondering if the front of her was as lovely as the back.

Then she'd turned around, and he'd realised she was lovelier than anything he could have imagined.

The sudden, visceral attraction that swept through him had rendered him literally speechless, and he'd stood there like a damned idiot, his eyes taking in her slender body bedecked in a simple white gown, her plump utterly kissable pink lips, her flushed cheeks, and her incredible, ice-green eyes.

How the hell was she still single?

It had all been going swimmingly, with Tristan enjoying the view and preparing to charm her. Something he found as easy as breathing.

Yes, it was going wonderfully well until he'd opened his mouth and told her who he was.

Never before had Tristan feared for his life from a mere slip of a lady. But he reckoned if the delectable Miss Gold had had a weapon in hand at that moment, he'd been fertilising the ground by sundown.

He frowned as he climbed atop his stallion, Odin.

As his head began to clear of the vision of Eleanor Gold, he thought further on their brief encounter.

Whilst the cottage had been prettily situated, it was barely bigger than the cottages of his tenants at home.

There had been no sign of a servant. And though the gown that he'd taken his time studying, mostly he had to admit because of what it was covering, was of good quality, it certainly wasn't the most fashionable.

Tristan's gut clenched painfully.

He had known, deep down, what he was doing to Augustus Gold's family.

When he'd heard of the scoundrel's demise, he could have left well enough alone. But no.

Vengeance had driven him to harden his heart and ignore the fact that he was no longer punishing Gold, but his children.

He hadn't cared. He'd been driven by an incessant need to take everything that had ever belonged to the man.

But what had he done, really? Forced those two young ladies into genteel poverty. The worst kind, he knew, because they couldn't work as the lower classes could to eke out a living.

And clearly they hadn't the means to get themselves to London and bag a husband to take care of them.

Tristan's stomach roiled as he faced the true consequences of what he'd done.

Worse still, even knowing what he'd done, he couldn't shake the desire that still heated his blood every time he thought of Miss Gold, with her bewitching eyes and hair that couldn't have been more fitting.

Tristan had planned to spend only a night or two in Torrell, look over the property, and then hand the matter off to his solicitors to take care of a quick sale.

Now, however, he felt compelled to stay around.

He didn't know quite what he wanted to do just yet. But he knew most definitely what he *didn't* want to do. And that was to walk away from Miss Eleanor Gold.

This was just as ridiculous as she had known it would be.

Eleanor's eyes practically rolled themselves out of her head as she took in the sight before her.

It was pretty, she had to admit. Distracting, too, which is what she'd wanted.

Everywhere she looked there were brightly coloured tents and caravans. Flags flying, a cacophony of shouts from "fortune tellers," and squeals from young, impressionable ladies like Pippa.

Trevor, when he'd come back from errands in their small village, had refused to come with them. He'd been spending a lot of time clearing the gardens around the cottage, and Eleanor didn't want to pull him away from the physical work that she thought helped him with his anger at the hand that Fate had dealt them.

She smiled bitterly at the irony of her turn of phrase.

It had been hands of cards that had ultimately gotten them into this mess.

Eleanor ran her gaze around the collection of caravans and people dotted around, listening mindlessly to Pippa's chatter, when her eyes alighted on one brightly covered conveyance and without conscious thought, she began to make her way to it.

Her feet moved of their own volition, as she felt an inexplicable pull toward the caravan. It was rounded as most gypsy conveyances were. Not particularly different to others in proximity.

Yet something about this one *called* to her, silly as that was.

Had Pippa said something so foolish, Eleanor would have teased her.

As she grew closer, a figure emerged and straightened, and Eleanor gasped as a hot sensation darted through her.

As she watched, the beautiful, exotic-looking woman gazed directly at her, her grey-blue eyes boring into Eleanor's.

Eleanor had the strange, not altogether pleasant feeling that the woman was looking *through* her, as though she could see into her very soul.

"And Miss Halloway said that the man was able to tell her the baron's *exact* age!" Pippa was rambling on, following Eleanor without paying any mind as to where they were going. "He was only off by about twelve years. Isn't that – Eleanor?"

As they drew closer, Eleanor glanced down at a painted sign.

Madame Zeta.

The name on that silly pamphlet Pippa had gotten from who knew where.

She looked back up and, this time, found herself studying the woman standing before her.

Though her eyes were the greyish-blue of a winter ocean, her skin was darker than almost any Eleanor had seen before, a beautiful honey colour. Her hair was jet black and ran down her back like a waterfall of a midnight, starless sky.

She was beautiful, but that wasn't her most striking feature.

It was the expression in her eyes. Eyes that looked like they belonged to someone ancient and wise, someone mythical. Hundreds of years old. And in them was a pain that Eleanor couldn't imagine someone ever feeling and living to tell of it.

Yet here she stood, back straight, chin proudly tilted. She had the carriage of a lady. Almost a queen. Right here in the middle of a gypsy camp.

"Ooh, that's Madame Zeta," Pippa whispered excitedly. "Please, do let's go in, Ellie."

Eleanor knew she should say no. That they

shouldn't spend their precious money on such things.

She didn't even believe in this sort of thing.

Did she?

Something inside her was compelling her to go inside. To have her palm read. Her fortune told.

But that was silly.

Eleanor shook her head slightly, taking a step backwards when her eyes snagged on the jewellery on Madame Zeta's neck.

There it was again, that strange, hot sensation. She felt as though it was almost pulsing from the talisman.

Without another moment's hesitation, she walked forward, stopping directly in front of the exotic, blue-eyed stranger.

She was acting strangely, Eleanor knew. And staring rudely at the piece.

"It is called The Path of Life."

Madame Zeta spoke in surprisingly cultured tones. Eleanor didn't know what she'd expected. Certainly not to be conversing with someone who sounded as if she could be gracing the drawing room of any house in the *haute monde*.

"What does it do?" she found herself asking, noting that she sounded a little breathless.

"Do?" Madame Zeta smiled gently. "It is but a necklace."

"What does it mean?"

"It represents the many different paths one can take, the many directions your life can go in. The centre circle goes on forever."

Eleanor looked up into Madame Zeta's eyes.

"It never changes. It is constant and permanent. No matter the path you take, the choices you make, the centre part, the part that is you—it is fixed. Circumstances may change for any of us, Miss. But the core of who we are? That is unchangeable."

Eleanor felt a sudden urge to cry. Madame Zeta's words brought more comfort than she could know.

No matter what had happened to the Gold siblings. No matter the choices they had made, and those that were made for them, they would always have each other. Always love each other.

The weight of the promise Eleanor had made to her siblings all those years ago sat heavily on her shoulders. So heavy sometimes, she worried it would crush her.

Yet her own path of life, though it had taken them every which way and far from what she'd imagined or wanted for them all, could never lessen the love she felt for her siblings, the desire she had to do right by them.

Silently, the fortune teller nodded her head toward the caravan.

She didn't pressure them. She didn't try to sell them any foolish spells, or speak to them in a nonsensical fashion.

She just stood placidly, quietly, patiently.

And though it was foolish in the extreme, Eleanor took a deep breath and swept inside.

Chapter Five

THE INSIDE OF the caravan was exactly what Eleanor would have expected it to be.

Covered in jewel-toned scarves, lit dimly by lanterns a plethora of shapes and sizes; it smelt exotic and intoxicating, putting Eleanor in mind of far off lands and people.

"Please, take a seat," Madame Zeta said softly, and Eleanor moved to a low stool situated across from where the woman was seating herself.

Pippa plopped herself down noisily beside Eleanor, her eyes wide, drinking in her surroundings.

"This is *marvellous,*" she whispered loudly.

Eleanor bit her lip, suddenly regretting her impetuousness. She didn't know what Madame Zeta would say, but she was quite sure she didn't want Pippa hearing it.

"Perhaps –" she began, but Madame Zeta interrupted her.

"My dear, you might allow your sister and I to speak privately. If you like, you may have your palm read after."

"O-oh." Pippa glanced at Eleanor, but Eleanor didn't argue with Madame Zeta. Instead, she sat guiltily whilst Pippa bustled around to remove herself. "Ellie, should I –"

"I'll be but a moment, Pip," she answered, imploring her sister to understand her need to hear whatever Madame Zeta had to say alone.

Pippa looked surprised but not upset.

"I'll just take a stroll around then," she said.

"Not too far," Eleanor called, earning herself an eyeroll.

After Pippa ducked out of the small wooden door, Eleanor felt inexplicably nervous.

Yet as soon as she met Madame Zeta's gaze, a sudden calm swept over her.

"Now—" The other woman smiled kindly. "Let us begin."

Eleanor held out her hand, palm up, and waited with anticipation for the other woman to start.

She studied her palm as Madame Zeta took it gently in her own, and was a little saddened by how coarsened the skin was.

It was vanity indeed to care so much about her hands looking work-roughened.

It was just, Eleanor supposed, outward evidence of how far they'd fallen. Of how she had failed to protect them all. Of how she had let them down.

"Things haven't been easy for you." Madame Zeta's

tone was so quiet, so reassuring. "You have not had the ease of life that you should have. That you expected."

Eleanor grimaced self-consciously. Having her inner thoughts echoed by this woman made her embarrassed by how selfish they were.

"You make me sound quite spoilt," she laughed.

The fortune teller looked straight at her, nothing but kindness and understanding in her eyes, alongside the sadness that seemed so much a part of her.

"There is no harm," Madame Zeta said, "in mourning the loss of the life we thought we would lead. When we have expectations, when we have hope, and it is cruelly taken from us, we are allowed to grieve. We are allowed to regret the hand that Fate deals us."

Eleanor blinked in shock at Madame Zeta's turn of phrase. It was just the one she had thought only moments before.

But it was Madame Zeta's previous words that really caught her attention.

They gave more comfort to Eleanor than she could have imagined. But more than that, the pain and regret in the other woman's tone made her heart clench painfully in sympathy and, without thought, she turned her hand over and squeezed the honey-coloured one in sympathy.

Madame Zeta smiled kindly at her then wordlessly turned her palm back over.

Eleanor studied the talisman around her neck

whilst Madame Zeta studied her palm, and once again that hot feeling spread through her.

The piece seemed to almost glow, even though it was a dull, aged gold.

Dull and aged gold. Just like her.

What a depressing thought.

Madame Zeta suddenly spoke again, and Eleanor had the uncomfortable feeling that the other lady was somehow able to read her thoughts.

"Yes, things have been tough for you, my dear. But they do not have to remain so. You have a kind heart and a quick mind. Do not let them be caught up in revenge and anger."

Eleanor couldn't help the gasp that escaped.

How could Madame Zeta know that she had felt little else but vengeance and anger since the odious Mr. Grayson had paid a call this afternoon?

"Sometimes it is hard to forgive the sins of the past. Some people allow themselves to get caught up in acts of revenge or unkindness. It blinds them to the good in front of them. It binds them to the bad. Do not let that happen to you, my dear."

"I don't –"

But Madame Zeta was not finished. Her words were flying out of her, almost as though she weren't in control of them. As though they were spilling from her of their own accord.

"A childhood enemy will return to your life. Do not

let his past sins colour your view of the future."

A childhood enemy.

Mr. Grayson.

Tristan Bloody Grayson.

All of her problems had begun with that man's connection to her father.

But why? That was one thing Eleanor had never stopped to wonder about until now. *Why* was Mr. Grayson the one to win every one of her father's properties? It almost seemed as though he were determinedly going after her father.

And if that were the case, what exactly had her father done to him to evoke such a strong reaction?

Eleanor felt slightly sick thinking about the possibilities.

But then, the sins of her father weren't hers. They weren't Pippa's or Trevor's, yet they were the ones paying the price.

How could she not let that colour the future?

Well, it was of no consequence now. She wasn't likely to see him again, so that couldn't be what Madame Zeta referred to.

Why had her mind immediately flown to him?

Because she didn't *have* any other enemies. Which just went to prove, all of this was poppycock.

Feeling suddenly frustrated with herself for being swept up in this, with Mr. Grayson for intruding on her thoughts and for having the gall to be handsome when he was such a terrible person, and with Madame Zeta for almost fooling her, Eleanor stood abruptly.

"I-I think that's enough now," she said. "Thank you for your time."

She dug into her reticule and pulled out a coin.

Wordlessly, she held it out to the fortune teller who remained seated.

She studied Eleanor's face for what seemed like an age before she reached out and accepted the coin with another regal nod of her head.

Eleanor turned to leave, feeling more frustrated than before she'd come to this silly caravan.

Before she ducked back out into the summer's afternoon, however, Madame Zeta spoke again.

"You know," she said softly, and Eleanor paused though she didn't turn back around. "The problems that cause you to lose sleep at night, the worries that weigh on your shoulders, they are fixable."

Eleanor whipped around to stare at the mysterious woman whose every word seemed to speak directly to her soul.

"Use your strengths, my dear. Do not hide from them. You do not have to follow in the footsteps of those who came before."

Eleanor smiled stiffly, thanked the fortune teller once more, and stepped outside the caravan.

She had no idea what that last part meant.

Use her strengths. Don't follow in other's footsteps.

The only strengths she had, really, were a capacity for numbers and, to her shame, an uncanny way with cards.

Her father had taught her when she'd been a little girl, before he'd become increasingly obsessed with gambling, and drinking, and whatever else he got up to in the various hells he attended.

But what good was any of that to her now?

Eleanor kept her head down, tired all of a sudden of the brightly coloured tents and shouts of laughter and excitement.

Her head was spinning slightly, and she felt nauseated. No doubt from the various exotic scents burning in the confined space of the caravan.

She would just collect Pippa and walk home.

The sea breeze by the cottage was sure to clear her head and –

"Miss Gold."

A very masculine and somewhat familiar voice called out to her.

Oh, no. No, no, no, no, NO.

Eleanor pretended not to hear and turned hurriedly to change direction.

"Miss Gold!"

Drat the man! Couldn't he see that she was avoiding him?

A hand grabbed Eleanor's elbow, and she screeched in fright.

"Ellie, you quite scared me to death!"

It was just Pippa.

Eleanor released her breath.

"Didn't you hear Mr. Grayson calling us?"

Eleanor finally noticed the large shadow looming behind Pippa, and she looked up slowly to see Mr. Grayson smiling down at her, looking like he didn't have a care in the world.

"What do you want?" she snapped, uncaring that she was ruder than she'd ever been to anyone in her life.

"Me?" He blinked innocently. "Oh, I merely wanted to follow women around all day shouting at them and having them ignore me."

Eleanor narrowed her eyes at him, including Pippa in her scowl, when her traitorous sister giggled behind her hand.

"Well, I'm glad you got what you wanted. Good day."

For the second time that day, she grabbed hold of her sister and manhandled her away from Mr. Grayson.

"Ellie, you're creating a scene," Pippa warned out of the corner of her mouth.

Indeed she was, yet she didn't care.

The Golds had grown up here. They knew everyone, save Mr. Grayson and the travelling fortune tellers in attendance here.

They knew Eleanor Gold wasn't the type to cause a scene for no reason.

They knew her shame at having to move from the only home here they'd ever known, to a tiny out-of-the-way cottage.

They knew she had no income.

They knew she was an on-the-shelf woman of five and twenty.

In short, there wasn't much humiliation left in her when it came to the residents of Torrell.

And she would rather embarrass herself in front of them all than deal with Mr. Grayson, in any case.

"Miss Gold, if I might have a moment of your time? Please?"

"Haven't you had enough from us, Mr. Grayson?" she snapped as she hurried away from him.

"That's what I wanted to talk to you about," he said conversationally, as though she weren't trying to run away from him in front of crowds of people. As though they were taking a pleasant stroll together in Hyde Park or something.

Eleanor decided the best thing to do would be to ignore him. If she ignored him, he would go away. For good, with any luck.

She marched poor Pippa along at a speed that very nearly killed them both, in total silence.

As for Mr. Grayson, well he chattered the *entire* way.

Some things were easy to ignore, even though she would have loved to hear about them in detail; his travels in India, his investments in new ventures.

Other things weren't as easy not to respond to; how pleasant Torrell was, how happily situated. How he would rather enjoy spending more time here.

Once or twice Pippa made to respond, but a squeeze from Eleanor ensured that her sister ignored him just as much as she.

After an interminable time, Tide Cottage came into view, and Eleanor breathed a sigh of relief.

The sooner they got away from this loathsome man, the better.

By the time they reached the front gate, Eleanor could have wept with relief.

Her shoulders were stiff from holding herself rigidly in check, refusing to respond, refusing to even look at him.

Refusing to notice how one stubborn lock of chestnut hair fell repeatedly over his brow, refusing to allow her hand to reach up and smooth it back.

And absolutely refusing to let her mind wander to how it would feel if he were to take her in those strong arms, if she were to turn her face up to his, if his head were to dip slowly toward hers and…

"Ellie."

"Yes? What?"

She snapped back to the present, cheeks burning to

see that Mr. Grayson and Pippa had stopped at the gate, matching looks of confusion on their faces, and she'd quite floated past it while her mind had been in the gutter.

That was his bloody fault.

Just about resisting the urge to stamp her foot, Eleanor marched back, grabbed hold of Pippa again, and then turned to propel them both up the path and to the door of Tide Cottage.

"Miss Gold, I really do want to talk to you. To explain –"

She didn't hear the rest of Mr. Grayson's words after she'd slammed the cottage door for the second time that day.

The man had taken everything from them.

What more did he want?

Chapter Six

"Y̲OU MOST CERTAINLY will *not* be going to any such thing."

Eleanor sighed as the world's longest day just kept on throwing things her way.

She had helped Mary to prepare a simple but tasty supper of rabbit stew and freshly baked bread, but the old servant wouldn't entertain the idea of the Gold children helping to scrub pots and clean up.

And so the three of them had been sent to the tiny drawing room as though they were still living in a grand house.

"Your house might have changed, but you are still Quality," Mary had said stoutly when Eleanor had tried to refuse.

Though it was mid-summer, the cottage could grow chilly at night, especially being so close to the sea, so Trevor had set a small fire in the hearth, and Eleanor had lit candles so they could read or sew.

They weren't at the point where they needed to conserve their candles. Not yet, in any case.

However, rather than read or sew, she was currently locked in a battle of wills with her tempestuous brother.

"But Ellie, I could win back some of it."

Eleanor wanted to scream at Trevor, to rail against his stupidity. But that wouldn't help.

He was at an age when he should be preparing to go out into the world, to have adventures and see wonderful sights before he settled into life as a landed gentleman.

And he wanted so desperately to be the man of the house, Eleanor knew. To take care of his sisters as a brother should.

But that wasn't possible. And certainly not this way.

Trevor had a lot of their father's impetuousness in him. Unfortunately, his talent for cards seemed to have been inherited from Mr. Gold, as well.

"Gambling is what got us into this mess in the first place, Trevor," she chided gently.

She'd been appalled when she'd found out there was some sort of den of iniquity between Torrell and the next, much larger town of Shepton.

Eleanor had always assumed her father did his gambling in Bath and in London, when the Season was open.

It made sense, she supposed, that he would have frequently gambled here in Torrell, too, to have burned through the vast wealth that had belonged to the Gold family for generations.

"I am not like Papa, Ellie," her younger brother implored her. "I know when to stop."

Yes, but you don't know how to play, she thought rather cattily.

It was true, though. Trevor had no talent for cards.

Nor did Pippa.

It was Eleanor who'd had an uncanny knack for them from infancy. Her ability to remember every card played, to add large numbers almost impossibly fast; it had always been a part of who she was.

"The pots are huge sometimes, Ellie. Really big. Even winning one or two would make such a difference to us, to our circumstances."

Even Pippa had dropped her sewing and was watching them now.

Eleanor could see the eagerness in Trevor's young face, the hope in Pippa's.

But the risk was too great.

The risk of gambling was always great, but for Trevor it was too big.

For Trevor…

An idea began to form in the back of Eleanor's mind. Foolish, silly, nonsensical.

She tried to push it away, but it was ruthless.

A small voice, growing steadily louder…

I could do it. I've never played a hand of cards I couldn't win.

But no. No! She would not be like her father, betting what little money they had. Risking being able to keep their heads above water.

But for how long? There is no income. Only the savings you've accumulated, and that will decline rapidly.

They would get work. Pippa could be a governess and, and Trevor could apprentice somebody somewhere.

And what about you? And Mary, whose loyalty has meant so much.

She wouldn't hear of it.

It was crazy. Foolish. She wouldn't entertain the notion for *any* of them.

"Well, what are we going to do for money then?" Trevor asked mutinously.

Eleanor stifled a sigh.

He was stubborn as a mule.

"We are doing just fine," she answered, the smile feeling brittle on her face.

"We can't go on like this forever, Ellie."

The soft interjection came from Pippa, and Eleanor's stomach roiled at the worry in Pippa's blue eyes, the frustration in Trevor's.

For so long she had tried to protect them from the harsh realities of their lives.

"We are not children," Pippa continued, as though she could read Eleanor's thoughts. "Most young women of my age are married or at least entertaining the idea."

Eleanor felt a wave of shame wash over her.

Yes, Pippa should be on the marriage mart. Trevor should be heading off to university soon.

But none of that was possible, and so they were stuck here at this awful impasse.

"I'm not saying I want to get married," Pippa said. "But we are soon to be four adults with mouths to feed and no income. How will we afford that?"

It was silly of her, Eleanor thought. Perhaps even unfair. To treat Pippa and Trevor like mere children. For they weren't. Nor were they stupid. How could she not have known that they would have the same worries as she?

"We shall have to work, Pip. That's all. Y-you can be a governess. And Trevor—" she turned to face her younger brother. "What would you like to do?"

"You know what I want to do," he answered quietly.

Yes, she knew. From the time he had gotten his first set of toy soldiers, Trevor had wanted to join the king's army. He wanted to be a commissioned officer as was fitting for a Gold.

"We can't afford to buy you a commission," Eleanor mumbled, shame colouring her cheeks.

"Not now, we can't," he snapped back. "But if I could –"

Eleanor felt her temper flare suddenly.

Today had been trying to say the least, and now this?

She knew that if Trevor had access to their coin, he would have gone off and bet it by now.

But Eleanor was in charge of the family accounts, and only Eleanor knew where she kept their funds. Not because she didn't trust her siblings, but because she needed to account for every penny of it.

"Trevor, you will not –"

A knock at the door interrupted what was sure to become an argument, and the siblings blinked at each other in surprise.

Only the vicar's wife had deigned to call on them in their new abode since they'd moved.

And that Tristan Bloody Grayson. Her father's moniker seemed appropriate now.

Their friends and the local villagers were still friendly, still kind. But as was usually the way with these things, embarrassment kept them from calling. Not knowing what to say kept them away.

"I'll get it," Mary hollered from the kitchen, before she ambled through the drawing room and into the small entryway.

Who on earth would be calling at night time?

"Mr. Tristan Grayson, here to see the Gold children."

Eleanor threw her eyes skywards as his smooth

tones infiltrated her somewhat peaceful abode.

She implored the Fates to ease off her a bit because, surely, they'd had their fun by now.

THE REDOUBTABLE MARY.

The butler retained at the manor house had explained in expressionless, unemotional tones that the woman who had acted as the late Mrs Gold's lady's maid had left the premises and was with the Gold children at Tide Cottage.

Tristan assumed that the stout, gimlet-eyed woman glaring at him now was she.

For a moment, he didn't think she'd let him in, but after appraising him from head to toe, she stepped back.

Nodding his thanks and receiving no acknowledgement of the action, Tristan stepped into the small drawing room.

His eyes ran swiftly over the room, and he felt what was becoming a familiar tug of guilt.

He had reduced the Gold family to this, for crimes that weren't their own.

Since earlier, he'd been replaying Eleanor Gold's bitter, angry words to him over and over.

"Explain how you took everything from us? How you ruined our lives as children and have continued to ruin

them right up until now? How you took from us the only home we've ever known? How you destroyed us and any chance of a future?"

He deserved the words. He deserved her censure.

But that didn't make them any easier to hear.

"You are a gambling cad like my father."

That one had been harder to swallow, but from her point of view, probably no less true.

It had been mere coincidence that he'd seen her again this afternoon.

He'd been wandering around the village, coming to terms with the place he would be staying for a while.

He had no intention of leaving until he saw right by Augustus Gold's innocent children.

And if he happened to see the beautiful Miss Eleanor Gold and spend some time in her company whilst he did that, well, that was just a happy quirk of the situation.

His eyes quickly landed on the object of almost every thought he'd had since he'd arrived in the bustling little village, and it wasn't his gut that tightened this time, base creature that he was.

Damn, but she was beautiful. How she had escaped the parson's trap, he had no clue. There wasn't a man alive who would take one look at her and care a whit about her lack of funds.

Add to that her razor-sharp tongue and spitfire

personality, and they should have been climbing over each other to get to her.

He found himself feeling happier than he should that she wasn't married.

Her unusual green eyes, eyes he hadn't been able to stop thinking about since this morning, were spitting fire at him right now, and damned if it didn't send a spike of lust through him.

Her hair was up now, he noted with some disappointment. And earlier in town, it had been covered by a delicate white bonnet.

And Tristan made a promise to himself there and then that he would see it unbound again, flowing down her back like a tumble of sunshine.

"Did you want something, Mr. Grayson, or has our palatial home rendered you mute?"

God, but she'd a tongue like a viper on her.

He was unable to suppress a grin at her icy disdain.

He'd glimpsed the fire beneath the coolly controlled surface. He knew she was a hell-cat underneath that ladylike stiffness.

"I wanted to speak to you—uh—all," he finished, finally able to drag his eyes from her to take in the pretty little sister he'd seen earlier and the angry-looking blond youth, who he assumed was her brother.

"Well, we are rather busy," she responded, not giving her siblings a chance to. "And in case I didn't make it clear earlier, *twice*," she emphasised, "We have no interest in you or anything you have to say."

Bloody hell, she was stubborn.

But so was he. And his conscience wouldn't allow them to live like this.

Tristan wracked his brain to think of something that would get through to her. Something that would make her listen.

"You need to leave."

His gaze darted to the boy. He had a mutinous set to his mouth like his older sister, though his eyes were blue.

A quick glance at the other Miss Gold showed that she seemed friendlier than her siblings, her eyes kinder. But she was most certainly not the one in charge, so was little help to him.

He turned to leave, frustration burning inside him.

Why wouldn't she bloody well listen?

Because of what he'd done to her father, and subsequently to them.

But what of what her father had done? He'd punished them for their father's wrongdoing, yes, but he was sorry for it. He was trying to fix it.

Tristan paused at that thought, and spun back around.

His gaze fixed only on Miss Gold again. It was almost impossible to notice anyone else in a room she was standing in.

Though she wasn't particularly tall, she held herself

like an Amazonian warrior woman—tall, proud, and protective of those in her care.

But who protected her? Who took care of her?

"Have you never wondered why?" he asked softly. "Why I was the one your father lost to time and time again. Why I was the one person who took everything that was his?

Something flickered in her green gaze.

Both her siblings turned to look questioningly at her. They would not react unless she did.

And she didn't.

With a sigh, Tristan turned back toward the front door and made his way into the cool night.

It would take more than paying a call to get through to her.

Eleanor Gold, he was fast learning, would not budge an inch lest she wanted to.

But neither would Tristan.

Chapter Seven

"WHAT DO YOU think he meant?" Pippa whispered, as though afraid to speak aloud, but it was enough to set them all into motion with Mary coming out from behind the door she'd clearly been eavesdropping at, and Pippa and Trevor moving to reclaim their seats.

Only Eleanor remained standing.

For try as she might not to care, she wanted to know what her father had done. Why, she couldn't say.

Perhaps some foolish part of her wanted to believe that Mr. Grayson had been misguided and angry, not cold and unfeeling, about what he was doing to her family.

"Who knows?" Trevor's tone was far too bitter for one so young. "I can only imagine when it comes to our father."

Suddenly, Eleanor's feet were moving.

She didn't want to imagine. She wanted to know. Needed to know the truth.

Without a word to any of them, she darted for the door and ran out into the night.

Mr. Grayson was just starting to climb onto his mount when she dashed into the yard.

He turned when heard her, and in the starlight she saw something flicker in his eyes, something that caused her breath to hitch.

But in an instant it was gone, and he walked toward her, stopping inches from where she stood, his face an expressionless mask.

"What did he do?" she asked, demanded really.

He studied her for an age, his piercing blue gaze running over her face, landing on her lips before moving back to her eyes.

"I have a lot I want to say to you, Miss Gold," he said softly, and Eleanor felt the sudden, mad urge to throw herself into his arms.

What on earth?!

"I don't have a lot I want to listen to, Mr. Grayson," she bit back, but her sudden breathlessness ruined the effect somewhat.

"Just tell me what he did so I at least know why you did this." She swept a hand back toward the cottage.

The truth of it was, Eleanor quite liked the cottage. It was growing on her by the day, and she couldn't have asked for somewhere more beautifully situated. Every day she awoke to the sound of the surf, the call of the gulls, and every window in the back of the house gave a view of the vast ocean.

She could happily live there forever if she knew that

Pippa and Trevor were well taken care of.

"I'm sorry," Mr. Grayson blurted out. "I'm sorry that you live here. That I've reduced you to this. I didn't—" He hesitated, and he looked so genuinely distressed that Eleanor felt a small, minute really, measure of sympathy for him. "I didn't know that Augustus's children were still at home, Miss Gold. I assumed – well…"

"You assumed that at twenty-five I, at least, would be married and taken care of," she finished for him, no trace of bitterness or anger in her tone. It was an understandable assumption.

"But you see, whilst you took the properties, my father did a good job of gambling away all his money. There was nothing, frankly, for me to Come Out. Even less for Pippa. And I've been so busy trying to keep us all from going completely under for the past five years, that finding someone to marry hasn't exactly been high on my list of priorities."

Mr. Grayson flinched as though she'd hit him.

"I want to help you," he said after an age, his tone hoarse. "I spent so many years focusing on exacting revenge on your father, I didn't or wouldn't see the damage I was doing to innocent parties. And I am truly sorry for that. But I can fix it. I can –"

"Mr. Grayson," Eleanor interrupted. *Fix it?* Her cheeks burned as she realised they were pathetic charity cases to him. Did her humiliation know no end?

"I came out here to find out what my father did. Not to have you sweep in and 'fix it'," she bit out angrily.

"I just wanted to do right by you, Miss Gold. To rectify –"

"To have us live off your charity, you mean." Her temper was flaring again. "Just tell me what he bloody well did."

He looked momentarily shocked by her outburst, but she was past caring.

"He ruined my father," he said, now, his eyes blazing with remembered anger. "He destroyed him at the gambling tables, and my father's heart never recovered from the shock of it. I've restored our fortunes, improved them even. I relentlessly chased down your father for years, taking everything I possibly could from him. But I can't get my father to walk again. I can't get him to talk."

Eleanor's heart raced as she listened to his dreadful accounting.

"You lost your house, Miss Gold, and for that I am more sorry than I can say. But I lost my father. Because, with the shell of a man he is today, he might as well be dead."

A heavy silence fell between them after Tristan's outburst, and he felt a sick sort of shame as he watched the colour drain from her face.

"I don't—" she began to stutter. "I didn't know. I'm sorry for –"

"Please don't," he interrupted.

He felt bad enough for what he'd reduced her to without her adding to his guilt by apologising for what her father had done.

He was aware of the irony of his feelings. He'd ruined them because of Augustus Gold but now, when she would take responsibility for that man's actions, he couldn't bear it.

"I've realised too late, Miss Gold, that seeking revenge was wrong. All I did was hurt you and your siblings. I want to make amends. I want to, to give you back your house."

He had thought she'd be pleased, but as he watched the moonlight play over her lovely face, he saw her tense, he saw her eyes narrow, and he saw a world of trouble coming his way.

"I've already told you," she bit out through clenched teeth, "we are not a charity case, sir."

"I know that," he snapped back, his own temper flaring. Why couldn't she just let him help?

Had he really only met her this morning? It felt like they'd been having this argument for years.

"Why won't you just let me bloody help you?"

"Why won't you leave us alone?"

An excellent question.

One that made him look too closely at his motivations.

Tristan didn't bloody well need this.

He was tired from all the travelling he'd done since he'd docked in London some weeks back, determined as he'd been to get this matter taken care of quickly and cleanly.

His guilt was gnawing at him, overshadowed only by the visceral lust he felt for this impossible woman.

He thought of the invitation he'd been subtly extended this afternoon.

A gaming hell in the next town over. Somewhere he could drink and, yes, play a few hands. Perhaps the apple didn't fall far from the tree.

But he never bet more than he could afford to lose. He'd learned his lesson the hard way. Still, there was something seductive about the thrill of the win.

He eyed the woman standing across from him, a combatant on the battlefield.

He could think of far more seductive things, but he was fond of his limbs and would like them to stay attached.

He'd tried, Tristan decided as he wordlessly turned to mount his stallion and get the hell out of there.

He didn't like lingering at this tiny cottage, knowing he was the reason they were living in it and he was unable to do anything about it because Eleanor Gold was an impossible, beautiful, wilful pain in the backside.

"You know," he called down from his horse while she scowled up at him, "Tonight I can enjoy a drink or two, the company of a far more pleasant female should the mood take me." He watched an endearing blush steal across her cheeks. He would never ordinarily speak to a lady thus. But this blasted woman brought out the worst in him. So he pushed ruthlessly on. "And a few hands of cards. I don't need to be here making amends. And you are letting that damnable pride get in the way of helping your siblings."

She opened her mouth to issue what would no doubt be a scathing retort, but he didn't stay to hear it.

He was going to go to that hell and distract himself from the woman with the face of an angel and the tongue of a devil.

ELEANOR SCREECHED HER frustrations to the night sky as soon as the figure of Tristan Bloody Grayson disappeared from view.

She never swore. Never. And look at her now, no better than a fishwife because of him.

She screamed again. But it didn't make her feel any better.

She *hated* him.

How dared he try to garner sympathy with the sad tale of his father and then offer to throw money and houses at her, as though that could undo the stress and worry and absolute chaos of the last five years? Ten years, really, since he'd first won against Augustus Gold.

But it was only when her father died that Eleanor took on the mountainous worry of the family's dire finances.

The cad. The odious, awful, horrible, *blackguard*.

She railed against the handsome Mr. Grayson in her mind, but it did nothing to calm the tempestuous hatred bubbling inside her.

He would trot off now and drink, and womanise (she chose to ignore what felt suspiciously like jealousy at this thought), and gamble. He wouldn't lose, either. He never lost, her father had once slurred this fact to her as he'd come home defeated again at Grayson's hands.

Eleanor's shoulders slumped as she began to slowly make her way inside.

He would lose if he should pit himself against her, though. She would love to wipe that smug smile from his face.

As soon as the idea formed, Eleanor stiffened, her head whipping up as her mind began to race with possibilities.

She couldn't. She *couldn't*. Could she?

No.

Oh, but the attraction of besting Tristan Bloody Grayson.

The feeling of coming home with pockets heavy with coin.

If the stakes were big enough and she played for long enough, she might even be able to purchase a commission for Trevor. He'd be settled. He'd be safe.

She might be able to raise some funds for Pippa to have new gowns. To go out to dances and parties.

Perhaps to find a husband.

But no.

How could she even contemplate it after what they'd lived through? After what gambling had done to their family.

Suddenly, the words of Madame Zeta came back to Eleanor, as though the honey-skinned woman were standing there whispering in her ear.

"Use your strengths, my dear. Do not hide from them. You do not have to follow in the footsteps of those who came before."

Was it true?

It couldn't be denied that she had a head for cards and numbers. More than anyone her father had ever come across, so he'd said.

Could she utilise her talent, earn some coin for her

siblings and herself, and *not* follow her father down a path of destruction?

Mr. Grayson's arrogant visage swam before her eyes, and Eleanor felt her resolve firm.

Yes, she absolutely could do it. And she would.

Chapter Eight

THIS WAS A lot less entertaining when his mind was filled with a green-eyed viper, Tristan decided some hours later.

He was sitting at a faro table, but his heart wasn't in it. He'd won every hand he'd played, but there was no real satisfaction in it. No challenge amongst these country folk.

And rather than revelling in the female companionship that he'd boasted to Miss Gold about, he found himself batting away the advances of more than one woman.

He'd every intention of spending a couple of hours with a woman. A brunette. As far from the golden-haired beauty as possible.

But it was no use.

He couldn't stop thinking about her, fuming at her, wanting her.

Tristan was just about to give the whole thing up as a bad cause and make the long trek back to Torrell, when a commotion at the door caught his attention.

He looked up, and his jaw hit the floor.

Standing at the front of the room, looking regal as a queen, was a masked woman.

She was wearing a cloak with the hood covering her hair and surrounding her face. And the mask she wore covered everything but a pair of delectable lips covered in rouge.

Tristan felt a tug of desire as he took in the sight of her.

Madness, since he couldn't see any part of her under the full cloak or the black mask she wore. Yet it was there.

The room had grown deathly quiet. It was obvious to every man there, including those in their cups, that this was no working lady.

The way she held herself, the way she moved as she snaked through the tables. She didn't belong here. Yet here she was.

He watched her, as did every other man in the place, as she sat at a table across the room from his own.

The men occupying that table half stood, clearly unsure of the protocol when a woman entered the gaming hell with the intention to play.

His eyes snapped back to the gruff, no-nonsense owner of the establishment. He was watching the lady but not moving to remove her.

He'd obviously given her permission to be here.

There was something unchivalrous about that,

Tristan frowned. Some of the players in here had taken him by surprise. They knew what they were doing, and they meant business.

It wasn't right to allow a lady to sit there and have her money taken from her.

Perhaps he should intervene and –

A cry of surprise went up at the lady's table, and he watched in astonishment as she won a rather sizeable pot.

Beginner's luck, perhaps. Or maybe the gentlemen at the table were distracted by the slender wrists and long, delicate fingers. The only part of the lady on display.

He watched closely, his own gambling quite forgotten, as he took in the lady's play.

No tricks that he could see. No cheating.

Bloody hell, she was good.

Another hand, another win for the mystery woman.

That odd, unexpected desire stirred in him again, Miss Gold almost forgotten in the face of the intrigue of the woman across the room.

She could handle herself, that much was obvious.

Tristan shook his head slightly and returned to the game at hand.

He couldn't get himself entangled with another female oddity.

But his desire to leave the hell had dissipated. He'd

hang around for a little while longer.

ELEANOR WAS SHAKING on the inside, but her hand was steady as a rock as she played hand after hand.

It was almost too easy to win against these drunkards.

She watched as they downed glass after glass of spirits, their speech slurring, their play becoming sloppier by the second.

When she'd first arrived, she'd almost bolted, giving this idea up for the fool's errand that it was.

But then she'd imagined Tristan Grayson's face as he pointed out how little she could do to take care of her siblings, and in she'd marched.

At first, the owner had point blank refused to allow her to enter.

After she'd promised him a quarter of her evening's earnings, however, she'd seen the curiosity along with the scepticism in his gaze.

He didn't believe that she had it in her to win.

Just another person to prove wrong.

She'd spotted Mr. Grayson straight away, of course.

Her eyes had travelled straight to him of their own accord.

It was an odd but pleasant sensation, knowing that she could see everyone and everything, yet they could hardly see her.

Being able to gaze directly at him, to look her fill of his impossibly handsome face, his strong, chiselled jaw, that lock of hair, without him knowing a single thing about her.

She saw the shock in his gaze, just like every other gaze in the place. She also saw the blaze of something else that she couldn't name but which made her feel decidedly hot and bothered.

But there was no time to think of such things now. Now she needed to get her head in the game and start winning some money.

There wasn't any room at his table, but she wouldn't play against him right away, in any case.

She wanted him to know how good she was. She wanted him to see her talent with his own eyes before she sat across from him and took every single penny he put on that table.

Her eyes flicked along the table, and she was confident she would win again.

Sure enough, the card flipped over, and Eleanor allowed herself a slight smile at the cacophony of groans, laughter, and appreciative cheers from the people who weren't losing hand over fist to her.

The thrill of the win coursed through her veins, but every time her excitement rose, she gave herself a stern talking to. A reminder of what their father had been. And she would immediately sober.

She wasn't here chasing an unachievable thrill. She was here to make money and take care of her siblings.

She darted a glance across the room to see that Mr. Grayson was watching her, in between insouciantly playing a card or two in his own game.

Their eyes met, and she watched his narrow, widen slightly then narrow again, this time accompanied by a clenching of his jaw.

Eleanor's stomach suddenly dropped.

He couldn't know it was her, could he?

She reached a hand up to pat at her hood, as casually as she could manage.

It was still in place. Not a tendril of her hair was on show; she was sure of it.

Perhaps her luck was about to run out, and something in Mr. Grayson's expression told her that her time was up.

Risking another glance across the room, Eleanor couldn't suppress a scowl as one of the ladies whose job she didn't even want to think about draped herself across Mr. Grayson's lap.

It didn't look as though he were particularly encouraging of the sultry brunette but still, it caused her more discomfort than it should.

It was time to get out of here. Eleanor placed her bet for the last hand she would play that night.

It was most of the money she had accumulated that night, and a low whistle went up somewhere behind her.

But she knew what she was doing.

She was confident that she would win. But if she didn't, if somehow the cards didn't go the way she expected, she would still walk out of there with slightly more coin than she'd come in with.

This wouldn't be for nought. The sickness, the nervousness, the arguments she'd had with Mary, who had realised what Eleanor was about when even Trevor and Pippa hadn't.

It would pay out because it had to.

The final card was flipped, and Eleanor released the breath she hadn't realised she'd been holding.

Without a word, she stood and nodded to the gentlemen surrounding her before moving swiftly to the door and the owner of the establishment.

There was a newfound respect in the man's eyes as she paid him his fee, as it were.

She didn't mind the arrangement, feeling sure that it lent her a level of protection, one that she would need if she were to attend a place such as this again.

Eleanor rushed through the shadows, her purse heavy with the evening's winnings tucked safely in a hidden pocket she'd hastily sewn into her cloak.

She'd tethered her mount as far away from others as she could manage.

A quick look around told her that nobody had followed, another worry that she had to contend with.

But it seemed she was alone.

As Eleanor rode swiftly and silently through the night, she allowed herself a grin of triumph.

Perhaps she hadn't gotten to play against Mr. Grayson tonight. But there was always next time.

Chapter Nine

Eleanor hummed to herself as she pottered around her garden.

For the first time in so very long, she felt light, young, free.

The vegetable patch was coming along nicely, and they were already enjoying produce from it.

That morning, she had sent Trevor and Pippa into the village. Trevor, to order meats from the butcher. Tonight, they would dine like royalty. Not every night, of course. She was still going to ensure they practised frugality and saved every penny they could.

But if she had many more evenings like last evening, she would be able to buy Trevor his commission by next year.

It was probably too late to look seriously into his schooling, though she insisted that he continue his studies at home. So she would concentrate on his commission.

Pippa had been sent to buy fabrics so she could sew herself some new gowns.

They'd both argued incessantly against spending so

much money, but Eleanor had insisted that she had it covered. Pippa's birthday was coming up and the meat, she said, would be for a celebratory dinner. The material a gift.

And so for the first time in a long time, her siblings skipped off happily, and Eleanor was able to watch them go and spend money without a knot of anxiety in her stomach.

Even Mary had gone to visit with the staff remaining at the manor house.

Eleanor knew that she would come back loaded with food from Cook, bought and baked using Mr. Grayson's money, but she couldn't care less. It was the least the man could do.

He did offer to give you back the deed, a voice whispered gently in her ear.

She was in no mood to listen to the voice that was on the side of Mr. Grayson.

Unbidden, an image of him staring at her across the room last night, watching as though he knew her secret, flashed into her mind, and she shook it away.

Of course, he hadn't known it was her. How could he?

"Good morning, Miss Gold."

Eleanor closed her eyes briefly as the now familiar voice of Mr. Grayson sounded above her head.

It was as though her mind had conjured the dratted man.

She ignored him, well aware of how outrageous her behaviour was.

Continuing her gardening with a renewed vigour, she listened for the sounds of his boots leaving her well enough alone.

There was no such sound, however.

"I understand I'm not your favourite person in the world, Miss Gold. But it's hardly fair to take it out on your vegetables."

Odious man.

Dropping the trowel, Eleanor prayed loudly for patience as she stood to face her tormentor.

"Tristan Bloody Grayson," she accidentally spat the moniker out loud before clamping a hand over her mouth.

She looked up into his face to see it go from surprised, to creased with amusement, no doubt at her praying, which she'd peppered with insults for good measure.

"That's not very Christian, Miss Gold," he chided laughingly.

If they weren't sworn enemies, Eleanor knew that she would be charmed by this incorrigible man, by his roguish smiles and wicked sense of humour, by the glimmer in his cobalt eyes, and the breadth of his impossibly large shoulders.

But they *were* mortal enemies, she reminded herself sternly. So she was beyond being charmed by him.

"Neither is stalking a woman who very obviously doesn't want your company, Mr. Grayson. Yet, here you are."

Lord, her mother would turn in her grave if she saw how abhorrently rude her daughter was being.

Yet Eleanor was beyond caring.

The longer she spent around this man, the more irresistible he was becoming. And that would not do.

She turned and began to untie her work apron as she made her way toward the back door of the cottage, one that would lead her to their small, serviceable kitchen and away from this man.

"Nor is gambling, my dear. Yet it didn't seem to stop you."

Eleanor drew to a halt as a snake of shock slithered down her spine.

She whipped around to stare at him, the apron now off and clutched in her hand.

"Wh-what did you say?" she asked. She should have sounded scornful, confused by his crazy question. But her voice shook, and she knew she must look guilty as sin.

"You heard me," he said softly, prowling toward her, a jungle cat stalking its prey.

Well, Eleanor would be damned before she backed away from him, so she stood her ground, albeit shaking like a leaf.

"I don't know what you're talking about."

"It took me a while," he said softly, as though she hadn't spoken. "To figure it out, I mean."

Eleanor could only swallow past the massive lump in her throat and stare at him.

"I was sitting there, and I look up, and a mystery woman walks in. I can't see any part of her, save her lips."

He reached out and ran a thumb along her lower lip, and the slow, wicked feeling that had been unfurling inside her since she'd first met him suddenly exploded and shot through every part of her.

"The most delectable, kissable lips I've ever seen." His voice became coarse and gravelly, raking over her fraught nerves.

"I felt – drawn to her, in a way I couldn't explain. After all, I saw no part of her. Except that mouth."

He stepped closer still, until there were only inches between them, and Eleanor had to turn her face up, her neck arched, just to keep looking into his eyes. She couldn't have looked away if her life depended on it.

He lifted his other hand, cupping the nape of her neck.

"All evening, as she won hand after hand, I wondered at it. This attraction."

He smiled, the grin wolfish, his eyes lit with blue fire.

"And then I realised something," he whispered, his mouth so close now she could almost taste his lips upon her own.

"What?" she barely managed to choke the word out.

"They weren't the most delectable lips I'd ever seen, for I'd seen a mouth that I was quite desperate to kiss just hours before then, felt that same desire coursing through my veins."

Eleanor's heart stuttered to a halt before racing quick as a butterfly's wings.

"I realised then that there couldn't be two women to whom I was so painfully, desperately attracted. Only one," he said softly, and Eleanor found herself aching for him to close the miniscule distance between them.

"Only you," he whispered before he captured her mouth in a kiss that sent her up in flames.

Tristan hadn't meant to kiss her, but nothing could stop him from doing so now.

As soon as his lips touched hers, the desire he'd been barely holding at bay roared to life, and he went up in smoke.

He felt her capitulate the second they touched.

Her arms snaked around his neck, her body, soft and pliant, pressed against his.

In some logical part of his brain, he knew that he shouldn't be standing in her garden, in full view of anyone who happened upon them, kissing her as though his life depended on it.

But all the forces of heaven and hell couldn't have made him stop. Not when she moaned her satisfaction and nearly floored him with the soft, seductive sound.

Not when his tongue delved inside her mouth and danced with her own.

He dragged his mouth from hers, trailed kisses along her jaw to capture one delicate earlobe between his teeth.

Her moans of pleasure would be the death of him, he was sure of it.

He moved to capture her lips once more, one hand keeping her face locked in place, the other moving to pull the straw hat from her head.

Just as he'd hoped, just as he'd imagined in the small hours of the night as he dreamt of her, her glorious hair fell with abandon around her shoulders, bombarding him with the smell of honeysuckle and *her*.

Pulling back slightly so he could take in the picture of her, soft and thoroughly kissed, hair like spun gold spilling down her back, eyes impossibly green and shining with a desire that only increased his own, Tristan felt a seismic shift inside him.

This didn't feel like mere lust, something that could be slaked by having her in his bed, though the thought alone made him groan with almost painful need.

No, he wanted her with more than his baser organs. He wanted to pit his wits against her. He wanted to see her bedecked in gowns and jewels. He wanted to dance with her, talk with her.

He wanted...*her*.

She was the most fascinating, irritating, entertaining, beautiful woman he'd ever met.

He felt more in two days in her company than he'd ever felt with a woman before. That had to mean something.

When he'd finally figured out what had been niggling at him about the strange woman sitting a room away from him last night, Tristan's heart had damn near stopped.

He'd been shocked, then scared, then furious.

Did she have any idea the danger she was putting herself in coming to a place like that alone? Any idea of the depths some men could sink to?

He'd meant to go over there and remove her, bodily if he had to, from the place.

But by the time he'd disentangled himself from the brunette with the seemingly never-ending limbs, Eleanor had gone.

He'd dashed outside to find her but hadn't seen a trace.

He had no idea what she was doing, but he'd been determined to come here today and tell her in no uncertain terms that she was to stop.

But then she'd been standing there looking more beautiful than his heart could stand, and that mouth of hers had spat insult after insult at him, and he couldn't help himself.

He needed to know if under all that tartness there was the sweetness he'd dreamed off, if under that ice-cold exterior there was the fire that he craved.

And damned if she didn't have them both in spades.

He kissed her again, softer this time, with less urgency, though it took all his self-control to keep himself reined in.

He didn't want to scare her with the power of what he was feeling for her.

He could do this all day. He could do this forever.

Keep her in his arms and protect her from all the world's harms.

That thought reminded him of why he'd really come here, and he reluctantly pulled away.

A smug, purely male satisfaction ran through him as he took in her dazed expression, her cheeks flushed from his kisses.

But before he lost the run of himself again, he needed to say what he'd come here to say.

"Eleanor," he started, hearing the lingering desire clinging to his words. "I don't want you going to that place again. It's not safe. I won't allow it."

Perhaps if he hadn't been so caught up in the web

of lust he was feeling, he would have noticed the warning signs.

As it was, he barely noticed her chin snapping up, her green eyes narrowing dangerously.

"Allow it?" she repeated softly.

"I don't think you realise the danger you put yourself in," he ploughed on, oblivious to the stiffening of her shoulders, the spark of fire in her eyes. "I've already told you, I'll gladly return the deed of the manor house to you."

He reached out and grazed his knuckles gently across her cheek.

"And you don't have to worry about money. Not anymore. I'll take care of you."

As he watched, Eleanor's cheeks paled dramatically before suddenly flushing bright red.

"Eleanor, what –"

"How *dare* you?" she hissed, not unlike their first meeting.

"What?" he asked, baffled by the fury stamped across her face. "Don't you understand? I'm offering to *help* you," he insisted.

There was a part of him that was a little insulted, if he were being entirely honest with himself.

Since his late teens, Tristan hadn't had to do much more than smile at a girl and she was putty in his hands.

This, having to work hard to charm a lady and still

being unsure as to how she felt about it, well it was different to say the least. He felt wrongfooted all the time around her, not something he was used to.

And now she looked angry. Furious, in fact. When he was offering to take away all of her problems, all of her worries.

"This thing between us," he spoke again, reaching out and clasping her upper arms. "I want to explore it," he said, expecting her to swoon any minute now.

Tristan frowned as he swept his gaze over her. He'd never seen anyone look less like swooning in his life, but there was still time.

"And I think you do, too," he smiled. "So, let me take care of the house, your funds. And we can concentrate on getting to know each other better."

Much as he was looking forward to getting to really know her, he was a base enough character to admit that he was looking forward to plenty more embraces like they'd just been enjoying.

He wasn't sure what he expected.

Gratitude, certainly.

Tears, possibly.

The resounding crack of her palm against his cheek? That was definitely unexpected.

Tristan couldn't contain the black oath that spilled from his lips as he pressed a hand to his stinging face.

Before he could question her, before he could do much of anything really, Eleanor had spun on her heel and marched inside the house.

The bang of the door and distinctive turn of the lock told him he likely wasn't welcome to go in after her.

Chapter Ten

Heaven preserve him from erratic, emotional women who should be carted off to Bedlam.

Tristan muttered furiously to himself as he untied Odin's reins from the post and prepared to return to the manor.

That was it. He'd absolutely had enough.

The solicitor could sell the damned house. He would offer compensation to the Gold siblings and be done with the whole sorry thing.

If she didn't take it, and she bloody well wouldn't, then that was her own problem. He would have done all he could.

He mounted the stallion and turned the horse toward the village.

Truth be told, he didn't particularly enjoy rattling around the Gold manor house alone. He couldn't think of it as anything other than Eleanor's house, and he hated the feeling of guilt that always accompanied that thought.

The servants had, he had to admit, started to warm to him a little.

Even the food was edible now.

But still, they didn't want him there anymore than he wanted to be there.

What the hell was wrong with the chit anyway? His mind bounced from thought to thought as his temper blazed hotter and hotter.

He didn't have to offer his help. He'd won the house, all of the properties, fairly and legally.

It wasn't his fault that their father was a dissolute wastrel. Hadn't his own been the same?

And, yes, Tristan had been lucky enough to be able to right the wrongs committed by his father. The Gold children didn't have the same opportunities, he knew.

As talented as Eleanor clearly was, she was restricted rather harshly by the fact that she was a female.

Her sister wouldn't fair any better, even if she weren't too docile to go out and fight for something.

The lad was too young to be of much use to anyone, at least for the next few years.

Tristan's temper began to cool as he thought of how dire the Golds' circumstances really were.

He'd been so angry with Eleanor for endangering herself last night once he'd realised who was beneath the mask.

Yet now that he thought about it, really thought it about it, he understood how few choices were actually available to the lady.

She could be a governess, he supposed, but he

doubted very much that she'd leave her siblings.

Besides which, any lady of his acquaintance would take one look at her and refuse to have her under the same roof as their husbands. He couldn't even say he would blame them. It would take a man far stronger, or blinder, than Tristan to not be tempted by Miss Gold.

But the truth was, there wasn't really anything else available for a lady of Quality who had fallen on hard times. Not when she had younger siblings to take care of.

If she were in Town or even Bath, no doubt she would be inundated with offers of affairs. Gentlemen would be lining up to offer her *carte blanch.*

They'd want to house her and dress her up as though she were a plaything kept for their amusements.

Tristan didn't necessarily abhor the practice. He'd had more than one mistress himself.

But he hated the thought of the clever, kind, prideful Miss Eleanor Gold being somebody's kept woman…

Tristan slowed Odin's fast pace as his mind replayed the disastrous conversation with Eleanor.

In light of what he'd just been thinking…

Surely, she didn't believe that he'd been offering –

"Damn and blast," he muttered as comprehension finally dawned.

What else could she have thought? He'd kissed her

senseless, admitted how much he wanted her, and then offered to give her a house and money and whatever else fool thing he'd said.

No wonder she'd slapped his cheek. He deserved far worse.

Tristan pinched the bridge of his nose.

What was it about this woman that constantly addled his brain, causing him to say the wrong thing?

Tristan was usually the suave, debonair rake that Society papers just loved to gossip about.

If they could see him now, they would think his foot had migrated permanently to his mouth.

There was no way to fix this that he could think of.

There was likely no way Miss Eleanor Gold would ever even speak to him again, let alone –

"Mr. Grayson."

At the sound of the lilting female voice, Tristan snapped out of his maudlin thoughts.

Coming toward him on a gig and pair that had seen far better days, was Miss Pippa and the youngest Gold, Trevor.

Tristan managed to paste a friendly look onto his face as the siblings approached.

He didn't think the gig would stop at all, but Miss Gold leaned in and whispered something to the boy, who reluctantly pulled to a stop.

"Good morning, Miss Gold, Mr. Gold." Tristan tipped his hat, earning himself a pretty smile and a scowl.

"Good morning, Mr. Grayson. Have you been at the cottage?" Pippa asked.

"Ah, yes, I called," he answered, unsure as to how much Eleanor would want her siblings to know. Not a lot, he would warrant. "But only for a moment or two. I have business in the village."

"Don't let us keep you then," the boy snapped coldly.

Miss Gold turned a look of displeasure on her brother, but Tristan didn't mind. The lad was protective of his sister, and God knew he had no reason to be nice to Tristan.

Not everyone was as good-natured and forgiving as Pippa Gold.

"Good morning, then." He tipped his hat once more and made to move off.

He hadn't even made it past the gig when Miss Gold piped up again.

"Mr. Grayson, I wondered, do you have plans for tomorrow evening?"

He turned his horse to face her.

"No, Miss Gold. I am quite free."

"Well then, I would like to invite you to dine at Tide Cottage with us."

Tristan could only gape at the young lady.

Didn't she know what he'd done? She didn't seem as though she were soft in the head but perhaps –

Miss Gold smiled as though she could read his thoughts.

"I am aware that I should see you as a sort of enemy, Mr. Grayson," the young blonde said quietly. "But I believe that our father wronged yours somehow, and I believe that you are sorry for your actions against us."

"I am," Tristan burst out. "I truly am."

"Just so." She nodded as though he'd given the correct answer. "And it would be far better for all of us, I think, if we could be friends rather than enemies. We are all victims of our fathers, one way or another."

The young lady's kind spirit and forgiveness put Tristan to shame.

Perhaps if he'd had even a fraction of her forgiving nature, the Golds wouldn't be in this position.

But then, he might never have met Eleanor Gold, and though their meetings thus far had been full of bitterness and arguments, excepting one explosive kiss, he wouldn't have it any other way.

Meeting her had been the most exciting thing to happen to Tristan in a very long time.

And now she would never speak to him again.

Of course, he thought, if she didn't want her siblings to know just what had gone on between them, she couldn't very well ignore him if he were to come to dinner, could she?

The smile Tristan turned on Miss Gold was genuine this time.

"I should be honoured to join you, Miss Gold."

He bade the siblings good morning and set off once more, his mood vastly improved.

Eleanor's head was aching by the time Pippa and Trevor arrived back from their shopping expedition.

Trevor's mood seemed dourer than usual.

But, Eleanor reasoned, he was a sixteen-year-old boy on the cusp of manhood. His moods were as changeable as the wind these days.

Pippa was filled with a nervous excitement as she showed Eleanor the fabrics she'd chosen for her gowns.

One, a white muslin sprigged with lavender. The other, a beautiful shade of the palest coral.

"These are lovely, Pip." Eleanor had smiled and hated the pang of envy she felt as she fingered the crisp, new fabric.

She was happy to get new gowns for Pippa. And if it meant that Pippa could go out into Society a little, after Eleanor had won them more money, then they would be worth it.

"I'm glad you think so," Pippa said, biting her lip. "For I bought enough of the coral for two gowns," she blurted out. "And—" she reached behind her and pulled out even more material, this one a plain white cotton "—I got this, too."

Eleanor opened her mouth to object, but Pippa spoke over her.

"I didn't spend more than you told me I could," she said. "And I thought that it would be better to get us both new gowns for the same money as you were willing to spend on just me. And we can design quite different dresses using both materials together."

Eleanor frowned at her younger sister before her eyes moved back to the new materials.

They truly were beautiful.

And it had been so long since she'd allowed herself to even think of wearing something new.

Pippa's skills with a needle were second to none, so Eleanor had no doubt she could make up some beautiful gowns.

Unbidden, Eleanor imagined what it would be like to face Mr. Grayson in a new, coral creation rather than her serviceable dimities and muslins she usually wore.

She hated that she even thought of him after what he'd said, what he'd thought of her.

She felt a sick shame burn through her.

How could he not think it? She wondered dully.

She'd gone to a gambling den alone in the middle of the night; she'd actually gambled whilst there. Then she'd allowed him to take liberties in the middle of the garden, in the middle of the day!

Not only allowed him to, but had fully participated,

had been seconds from begging for more.

And most likely would have if he'd not opened that idiotic mouth of his and said, well essentially said that he would pay for her favours.

Rage battled with humiliation until she could barely speak with the emotions roiling inside her.

Taking a deep, calming breath, she reached out and took her sister in a tight hug.

"Thank you, dear," she said. "I love the material, and I love that we shall both get to wear new gowns. Now, let's help Mary prepare that lovely duck that Trevor brought back."

"Um, d-do you think we could have something simpler today, Ellie? I don't feel terribly well. Anything too rich will likely make me feel sick."

Eleanor eyed Pippa and was alarmed by the girl's sudden pallor.

"Of course, Pip. You are pale. Why don't we take a quick walk by the sea and when we come back, we'll get started on those dresses. The duck will keep until tomorrow."

"It will indeed." Pippa grinned as she jumped to her feet, looking much better all of a sudden. "Let's go."

"ELLIE, PLEASE BE reasonable."

"Reasonable?" Eleanor practically screeched as she

faced her sister across her small bedroom. "Inviting that, that *cad* into our home and not even telling me about it. Is that reasonable?"

Eleanor was shaking as she darted another look at the ormolu clock on her mantle.

Thirty minutes.

In just thirty minutes Tristan Bloody Grayson would be in their house. Expecting to be fed no less!

The audacity of the man. To accept an invitation after what he'd said. What he'd implied.

It was the outside of enough.

The worst of it was that she'd been helping to prepare the blasted dinner party all day.

When Pippa had suggested they give the small dining room a good clean, Eleanor had attacked the space with gusto. She'd even enjoyed the chance to burn off some of the nervous energy she'd been left with after that kiss the previous day.

Then, Pippa had suggested they make food fit for a dinner party for the evening meal, and Eleanor had been so happy to see Pippa excited and not worrying about anything for once that she'd joined in.

Trevor had been making himself scarce for most of the day, but he did so often, and Eleanor hadn't thought anything of it.

Now though, with only minutes to go until their guest's arrival, Pippa had confessed all. And Eleanor found out that Trevor was making himself scarce because he wanted Mr. Grayson here even less than she did.

Well, she hoped Pippa enjoyed hosting because Hell would freeze over before Eleanor sat across the dinner table from that man.

Tristan tethered Odin and straightened his jacket nervously before walking up the small, stone path to the door of Tide Cottage.

He was being ridiculous, he knew. Acting for all the world like a debutante at her first ball. But seeing Eleanor again after that kiss, and then that—unfortunate incident—made him more anxious than a green lad.

But he had been invited. And though he'd half expected a note to arrive today, the invitation hadn't been rescinded. Which must mean that she wanted him here. Or would at least tolerate his presence.

Well, he could delay no longer. The sooner he got inside, the sooner he would see her and could begin to make amends. Again.

Eleanor worked hard to keep her expression impassive as Mary showed Tristan into their drawing room. She didn't know when she'd started thinking of him as Tristan and not Mr. Grayson, but after their – intimacies – there seemed little point in sticking to that particular formality. At least in her head.

He'd been here once before, of course, but she hadn't been as aware of him then. She hadn't felt the strength in those muscled arms, felt the power in the broad shoulders. Now, the room seemed to shrink around him.

Eleanor had only swept into the room seconds before he'd knocked upon the door.

She'd sat upstairs, mutinously refusing to come down.

But Pippa rarely if ever asked for anything, and she'd begged Eleanor to join them.

So with only minutes to spare, Eleanor had donned her only halfway decent gown, a pale sage satin that was the perfect foil for her green eyes and golden blonde hair.

She hadn't left herself time to do anything other than pile her hair atop her head and affix a satin ribbon in the same shade of the dress.

A pair of white evening gloves finished the ensemble, and whether or not she looked well put together, she was here.

Pippa jumped to her feet and moved to greet the intruder warmly.

Even Trevor issued a stiff but well executed bow.

Finally, it was her turn.

She dipped a small curtsy, refusing to hold her hand out to him, and refusing to speak.

Neither of which put him off.

He reached out and grasped her hand anyway, bowing over it and placing a blazing hot kiss on it, which she felt through the glove, and right the way up her arm.

"Miss Gold, you are enchanting," he said softly and as their eyes connected, his burned with the blue flame of desire, while an answering fire raged to life inside Eleanor.

She snatched her hand back and moved to take her seat.

Let Pippa carry the conversation for the evening. She had been the one to invite Tristan in the first place. Eleanor wouldn't speak a word to the man. Not a single word.

Chapter Eleven

"But surely you miss it? The excitement, the adventure?"

Tristan could barely keep his train of thought as Eleanor gazed across the table at him, her eyes blazing with excitement as he regaled them with tales from his life in India.

He felt quite sure that she'd made some sort of oath not to speak to him, for when he'd first arrived he'd have fared better trying to extract blood from a stone, than trying to get a word out of Eleanor.

As dinner had been served by their maid, however, and Pippa had asked him about his business interests in India, Eleanor had grown more interested. He'd known by the way she listened intently to what he said, how she leaned forward in her seat slightly as he told them of a storm he'd been caught in on his way across the ocean.

Eventually, she'd begun to ask questions. Intelligent, interested questions, and he'd found himself thoroughly enjoying this small, informal dinner party.

Even Trevor had warmed to him when he'd mentioned that a cousin of his was an officer in the army.

"I want to be an officer," Trevor had said, his eyes shining, and Tristan had caught the look that passed over Eleanor's face. A strange mix of regret, pride, and determination.

This then, was why she was risking her reputation, and more besides, by attending gambling dens.

He hated the idea of it, and yet when he'd tried to interfere earlier he'd earned a smack for his troubles.

The younger Miss Gold, he'd been informed, wanted nothing more than to get married and live a quiet life in the countryside. She would probably end up as a governess somewhere, she continued pragmatically and again, that flicker of emotion on her sister's face.

Tristan secretly thought that Pippa Gold was likely to run into the same problems as her sister. She might not quite have Eleanor's beauty, but she was uncommonly pretty, and he would stake his life on the fact that she didn't have anywhere near her sister's gumption. Eleanor would be able to handle herself in a difficult situation.

He didn't think the same could be said of Pippa.

And that bothered Tristan, too, for different reasons.

Jealousy, protectiveness, and something else indefinable drove his feelings for Eleanor Gold. He would happily tear apart limb from limb any man who laid a finger on her.

With Pippa, he felt as a protective older brother would.

It was most disconcerting.

It must be lingering guilt over the conditions in which they were living. Frustration that Eleanor wouldn't allow him to help.

But while they all chattered about India, and the army, and a plethora of other things, Tristan was thinking only of Eleanor and her determination to place herself in harm's way to provide for her siblings.

"Ellie—" Trevor spoke up during a lull in the conversation whilst they finished a delicious peach pudding. "The – ah – matter we discussed the other day. Father's old friend Sir Bernard is in town on Friday. I thought –"

Eleanor's green gaze darted to Tristan and back to her brother.

"No," she said firmly.

Trevor's cheeks grew hot, and Tristan recognised the signs of a young man losing grip on his temper.

"But –"

"No, Trevor." Eleanor spoke with quiet finality. There was a slight pause whilst Trevor stewed, then she spoke again. "Friday?" she asked, and Tristan glared at her across the table.

Trevor merely nodded, and Tristan's own temper grew as he watched her victorious smile.

She glanced his way, and he made sure to deepen

his scowl. She raised a brow, and he could almost hear her asking what business it was of his.

And it really wasn't any of his business. Logically he knew that. The problem was that logic tended to desert him around this woman.

He couldn't stop her from going.

But he could make sure that he was there.

IF MR. GRAYSON thought that glaring at her across the room was going to intimidate her, or force her to leave, then he was very much mistaken.

Eleanor could feel his eyes boring into her, but she steadfastly refused to meet his glare.

She had been more pleased than she cared to admit when she'd walked in this evening and seen him there.

He wasn't at one of the tables, but merely standing at the bar scowling ferociously at anyone who came near him.

Clearly he was in a towering rage. What was less clear was why his mood was so dour.

After all, they'd known each other only four weeks. What she did, the actions she took, had nothing to do with him.

It had been thus since their dinner party three weeks ago. When Trevor had informed Eleanor that an old acquaintance of their father, who was as fond of throwing his money away as his old companion had been, was going to be at the hell, she had been determined to win a tidy sum from the man.

And she had. So she kept coming back. Every Friday. And every Saturday morning she awoke a little more well off than she had been the morning before.

And throughout it all, Tristan Bloody Grayson tried to put her off. He came to dinner frequently, at Pippa's invitation.

He showed up in the village when she was shopping.

He showed up on the beach when she was walking, or in the woods when she was riding.

And every time they spoke alone, he tried to convince her to give up her gambling. Every. Single. Time.

Now, here he was watching her, narrowing his eyes at every other player at her table, fussing like an overprotective mother hen.

It was quite off-putting, and had Eleanor been playing against anyone with real skill, she would have been in trouble.

As it was, the calibre of gambler this week was the same as last, and so she was making a tidy sum with every hand she played.

Eleanor turned her attention back to the table at which she was sitting, casting a quick glance around the men sitting there.

Their expressions ranged from irritated to baffled.

Only one gave her pause.

Her eyes alighted on those of a gentleman she didn't recognise, and the sheer loathing that blazed from him made Eleanor recoil.

A snake of fear slithered down her spine as he leered at her.

He looked angry, yes. But there was something else. Something that turned her stomach.

Perhaps it was time to leave.

Just as Eleanor was readying herself to go home, the stranger spoke, his voice slurred with alcohol, his tone spiteful.

"What's a pretty little thing like you doing gambling at these tables?"

Eleanor's stomach clenched uneasily, but she held her composure.

Given that she was completely covered, save for her mouth, the man had no way of knowing whether she was "pretty" or not.

"Winning," she answered stubbornly, earning a round of laugher.

The stranger didn't laugh, however. His scowl deepened.

"I don't like losing to a woman," he said now, spittle flying from his mouth.

"I suggest you learn how to play cards then," she bit back.

Standing before he could make her feel even more

uncomfortable, Eleanor nodded a general goodbye to the men seated at the table.

For the most part, they bade her farewell. Some even standing.

After they'd gotten over the shock of a woman in their midst who wasn't there to – service them – Eleanor balked at the idea, but it was what it was and she couldn't come to a gaming hell and not expect to see it – the men had been, if not friendly then at least civil.

Not this man, though.

This man's anger and disgust were palpable.

Eleanor darted her gaze across the room, but Tristan was gone.

She frowned her disappointment. What did she care what he did?

A small part of her had to admit that his presence would have made her feel safer. But it wasn't his job to protect her, and she wouldn't have wanted his interference, in any case.

She had been more pleased than she had any right to be when she'd watched from the corner of her eye as he'd rejected more than one advance from the women working in the hell.

After that, she resolutely avoided looking over there. Because Tristan Grayson shouldn't concern her. *Didn't* concern her.

Without another thought for her nemesis or the

grotesque man attempting to frighten her, Eleanor moved swiftly toward the exit.

Moments after concluding her dealings with the hell's owner, Eleanor made her way toward her mount.

The night was unseasonably cool and she shivered slightly as she pulled the cloak tighter to shoulders.

It made her uneasy, being alone. Certainly more uneasy than she'd been last time.

But she was being silly, of course.

Nobody knew who she was, so there was no risk to her reputation.

Perhaps naïvely, she trusted Tristan with her secret and somehow knew he would never betray her.

She couldn't risk anyone finding out who she really was.

If Trevor were to become a respected officer, and Pippa were to be gently reintroduced to Society, Eleanor needed to make sure not a whiff of scandal tarnished the Gold name. It would be hard enough to get people to accept Pippa after what their father had been. Add a gambling sister who actually attended gaming hells, and Pippa wouldn't even be taken on as a governess.

The distinctive sound of gravel crunching underfoot came from behind Eleanor, and she spun around to examine the darkness.

She couldn't see anything, but she had the distinct impression that she was being watched.

The sooner she got to her mount and set off for home the better.

For the first time, Eleanor wondered at the cleverness of her plan. Anything could happen to her, either in there or out on the road alone in the middle of the night.

Even if it was nothing nefarious. Even if her horse came up lame. She could be stranded, quite alone and without the means of attaining help.

It was a sobering thought and one she hadn't really considered before.

The temptation of winning so much coin, of dragging her family from the brink of utter ruin to perhaps allowing Trevor and Pippa the freedom to have the lives they wanted, and not that which was forced upon them, had been too much to resist. And so she'd thrown caution to the wind.

Perhaps she was more like her father than she'd thought.

So distracted had Eleanor been by her thoughts that her mind wasn't on her surroundings.

When a hand suddenly reached out of the gloom and wrapped itself around her throat, she didn't even have time to scream.

She felt herself being dragged backwards toward a body whose stench almost made her gag.

And the voice that suddenly sounded in her ear was, she knew, that of the man who'd filled her with dread in the gaming hell.

"You need to be careful carrying all that coin about, Missy. There are all sorts of bad-meaning folk around here."

"Let go of me," she gasped, trying and failing to sound strong and courageous, and not sick with fear.

"You can have your money back," she managed to gasp out while the arm that wasn't holding her neck wrapped around her waist.

"I suddenly find that it's not your money I want." He laughed, and the sound put a fear unlike anything Eleanor had ever felt straight into her heart.

Chapter Twelve

Surely it shouldn't take her this long to get to her horse.

Tristan frowned as he consulted his timepiece once more.

It was difficult to see. The night was cloudy and the moon weak.

But he knew that more minutes had past than should have for Eleanor to make it from the front of the establishment to the horse that she'd rather foolishly left isolated.

Tristan knew men. And he knew a lot of them couldn't be trusted. Especially when they were thoroughly foxed and felt slighted.

He'd watched the short but tension fuelled conversation between Eleanor and the man who Tristan hadn't liked the look of from the moment Eleanor sat at that damned table.

Though he couldn't hear what was being said, he could guess well enough. There were rumblings around the hell. And the men weren't happy that there was a lady amongst them. Less happy that she was whipping them and costing them a small fortune with that quick mind of hers.

He'd never seen anyone play cards like she could. He'd be impressed by her if he weren't so damned worried.

The second she'd moved to leave, so had Tristan. He was determined to follow her both to the place and from it, every time she insisted on going.

She didn't have to be happy about it, but at least she'd be safe.

Or so he'd thought.

His heart hammered as he consulted the timepiece again. Even allowing for the time it would take her to consult with the owner, she should be here by now.

That was it.

He was going back.

Somewhere in his mind Tristan was remembering his determination to leave Torrell as soon as he'd checked over the manor house. Some part of him was wondering why, after only a few blazing arguments and one sensational kiss, he was determined to stay and be in Eleanor Gold's life whether she wished him to be or not.

He ignored that part of him. Because he didn't want to examine the reason why. He was fairly confident that it would change him permanently and irreversibly.

Tristan was just passing a darkened alleyway at the

side of the building when a sound caught his attention.

What was that? It had sounded like –

A woman's screech rent the air, and an overwhelming fear hit him square in the gut.

Without a second's hesitation, he raced down the alley toward the sound.

At the sight that met him, his fear was replaced by an incendiary anger.

The hood of Eleanor's cloak had fallen down, and her hair shone golden in the pale moonlight.

But that wasn't what caught Tristan's attention.

The fact that she was standing pressed against the stone wall of the alley with a filthy hand at her throat was the only thing Tristan saw, the only thing he could see.

He watched as she pulled and clawed at the hand but it was unmoving.

A growl of rage escaped him, and Eleanor's eyes whipped to him, as did the face of the bastard who was attacking her.

Tristan didn't look at her. Couldn't risk being distracted by her.

He slammed himself into the man until they both crashed to the ground.

Tristan's anger fuelled him, and the unnamed man didn't even have a chance to right himself before Tristan was upon him.

"I'll kill you," he promised and felt a surge of satisfaction as the man's bloodshot eyes filled with terror.

"Stop."

He barely heard Eleanor's whispered plea as he slammed his fist into the drunkard's nose and rejoiced in the sound of crunching bones.

He'd never before had a bloodlust like this. Though he regularly attended Gentleman Jackson's when he was in Town, Tristan had never particularly had a penchant for violence or fighting.

Right now, though, he could happily watch the life drain from the blackguard beneath him.

He pounded his fist into the assailant's face and would have continued if Eleanor hadn't spoken again.

"Tristan," she sobbed, and even through his anger, his gut clenched with agony at the fear in her voice. And that, of course, angered him further still. "Please," she cried. "Please, stop."

Nothing else could have made him. No one else would have gotten through the raging emotions swirling inside him.

But she did.

He climbed to his feet, dragging the bastard with him.

"You've broken my bloody nose," the man shouted, and Tristan tightened his grip on the fellow's coat.

It wasn't an overly expensive coat, but it wasn't the rough material favoured by the working classes, either. At a guess, Tristan would say he was a merchant or farmer who did well for himself.

"I'll break every single bone in your sorry body if you ever touch her again," Tristan promised, his voice icy and all the more lethal because of it. "I'll find out who you are, and I will destroy you."

The man said nothing, but his rapid nodding seemed to indicate that he knew Tristan meant every word of his threat.

He shoved the blackguard away and watched as he stumbled down the alleyway and out of sight.

That left only Tristan and Eleanor.

He took a steadying breath, willing his hands to stop shaking before he turned back around to face her.

She's safe, he told himself over and over again. *She's safe and unharmed.*

And most likely scared out of her wits.

He'd never lost his temper like that in front of a female. He'd never felt the loss of control like that before, at all.

And she would be terrified of him now. She would probably never want to see or speak to him again.

He turned slowly to face her and made sure he kept his distance, cursing his bloodied hands as he dropped them to his sides.

He would have to try somehow to reassure her that she was safe with him so he could get her the hell out of here.

"Eleanor," he spoke calmly, softly.

He hated the look in her eyes. It was haunted as she gazed at him wide-eyed. He'd never seen her look scared before, and it made him want to hunt the bastard down and carry out his threat.

"Did he hurt you?" he asked, knowing that if her answer was yes, nothing, not even she, would stop him.

She didn't answer him. Didn't move.

"Eleanor," he repeated and took a small, slow step forward. "Sweetheart."

With a sob, she suddenly flew at him, throwing herself into his arms and burying her face in his chest.

He felt a moment of shock before the feel of her clinging to him, and the knowledge that he was holding her and she was safe washed over him. He wrapped his arms around her, pulling her closer, burying his face in her hair, inhaling the floral scent that drove him wild.

It felt right, holding her like this. His heart thudded with the knowledge that this was where she belonged. Right there in his arms.

ELEANOR COULDN'T STOP herself from shaking.

Try as she might, she just couldn't seem to get warm. It felt as though the cold snap of fear had seeped into her very bones.

When she thought of what might have happened –

She shuddered and saw Tristan's concerned gaze snap over to her.

He'd wanted them to share his horse, assuring her that he could manage to keep hold of the reins of her docile mare.

But Eleanor had refused, tempting though the offer was.

He'd immediately acquiesced, a first for him.

No doubt he thought she was too traumatised by what had happened to want to sit for over an hour in a man's arms.

Well, she was happy to let him think that, though nothing could be further from the truth.

The problem was that there was nowhere else she'd rather be than in his arms.

And it wasn't just because he'd rescued her, though she had been more relieved, more grateful than she would ever be able to say that he had come when he did.

Ordinarily she would have been furious that he was dogging her movements, watching her and treating her as though she were helpless and incapable of taking care of herself.

She had never thought, not in her worst nightmares, that he would be absolutely correct.

She'd never been more scared in her life as she'd been down that alleyway. And though she was an innocent, she was still twenty-five. Plenty old enough to know exactly what that animal's intentions had been.

Eleanor risked a glance at Tristan and saw that he was watching the road ahead. But his jaw was clenched and the knuckles that weren't bruised and swollen were white as they gripped the reins of his stallion.

Was he angry with her?

She'd never seen anyone as furious as he had been back there. For one, sickening moment she had thought he wouldn't stop when he was beating the man to a pulp.

But he had stopped. He'd stopped, and he'd comforted her. He'd let her cry herself hoarse in his arms.

He hadn't railed against her for her foolish naïveté. He hadn't pointed out that he'd warned her about the dangers of her actions.

For as rough and violent as he'd been with her attacker, he had been nothing but gentle and careful with her.

She appreciated his silence, too. Her head was running riot with so many emotions and feelings, she was worried it would spin clean off.

Every time she thought of what had happened, she felt dread, nausea, disgust.

Every time she remembered the look of hatred and triumph in that man's eyes, she felt revulsion.

More shocking, though, and she was quite sure terribly inappropriately, she felt a swell of desire and tenderness when she remembered Tristan rushing to her rescue. Something she couldn't even begin to understand.

They rode in silence interspersed with his questions about how she was feeling, if she was sore, if she needed to stop, if she were warm enough.

But it wasn't an uncomfortable silence. Or if it was, Eleanor didn't notice.

She was in shock, she knew; her teeth chattering, her head pounding. Tristan had tried more than once to hand over his jacket, but Eleanor had refused.

For one thing, it wouldn't make a difference and for another, if she were surrounded by his scent like that, she was likely to fall of her horse at least once, and she just wanted to get home.

Still, deep down inside, wrong though it was, she relished the time with him. Being alone in the quiet, still night.

If the circumstances had been better…

And just like that, her mind flew to the attack in the alleyway, and her feeling of comfort and even happiness was chased away once more.

By the time Tide Cottage appeared on the road in front of them, Eleanor was exhausted, sick, sore, and determined.

She'd been thinking on what to do this past half hour, and though she wasn't thrilled at the prospect, it really did seem the only way.

They came to a halt in the small yard of the cottage, and Eleanor watched as Tristan took charge as though he owned the place.

But she was too tired to raise any sort of objection and besides, it felt nice to be looked after. She had been the one doing the looking after for so long, it was comforting to allow herself to be taken care of.

Tristan lifted her from the horse, and her heart raced as his strong hands wrapped around her waist.

He held her as though she weighed nothing and for one glorious, mad moment as he placed her on her feet and his cobalt gaze locked with hers, she thought he would kiss her. She *wanted* him to kiss her.

Tristan's kiss would chase away any other thought in her head, unpleasant or otherwise.

But after a tense moment, he shook his head gently and moved away to take care of the horses.

She followed at a slower pace as he moved toward their makeshift stable and made light work of removing the saddle from the mare and settling the horse in for the night.

When he was done, he walked slowly toward her.

"Are you well?" he asked, his face the picture of concern.

That chestnut lock fell across his brow once more, and Eleanor's fingers itched to brush it away.

Instead, she smiled tiredly.

"I am," she assured him for the hundredth time.

She hesitated before speaking again.

"Tristan," she began, not even noticing that she'd slipped into calling him by his first name. "I – back there when –" She swallowed a lump in her throat. But she would not cry again. Not until she was safely inside her bedchamber and alone. "Thank you," she finally uttered, gazing up at him, hoping he could see the depth of the gratitude she felt in her eyes. "I am more grateful to you than I can say."

He reached out and grazed his knuckles softy across her cheek. Thankfully not using the hand that had punched the living daylights out of her assailant.

"I'm just glad I was there," he said, his eyes burning with an emotion that made her breath hitch. "If I hadn't gotten to you –" He cut himself off as a look of intense pain skittered across his face.

"But you did," she assured him, reaching up and taking his hand in her own, squeezing it gently. "You did. I am safe because of you."

He placed a soft kiss on the back of her hand, and her blood heated from that merest of touches. She didn't want him to leave, Eleanor realized. Yet she needed to be alone, to try and process everything that had happened tonight.

"Thankfully it's all over now." He smiled as he released her. "You can rest tonight and try to put it all behind you."

Eleanor nodded in agreement.

"Next time, I will ensure that I take more care," she said softly.

Tristan stiffened, his face blanching. "Next time?" he asked softly, lethally.

"Why, yes." She frowned at his odd behaviour. He suddenly seemed *furious*.

"I'll take much better care," she confirmed. "When I go back."

He took a step toward her, so close that she could feel the tension emanating from him.

"Like hell you will."

Chapter Thirteen

ELEANOR TRIED TO slam the door in the arrogant brute's face, all tender feelings well and truly gone.

All she managed, however, was to bang it off the foot that he'd stuck in the doorway.

She stomped into the kitchen, turning to glower at him as he stepped into the small room and swamped it with his ridiculously oversized shoulders.

"Do *not* presume to tell me what to do," she whispered furiously. Oh how she wished she could shout and rail against him, but she couldn't risk waking Mary and her siblings.

"Have you lost your damned mind?" he bit out, and she gasped in afront. "After what happened to you tonight, you would go back there?"

"Yes, I would. I *will*," she bit back stubbornly.

He suddenly reached out and grasped her upper arms, shaking her gently.

"Eleanor, do you have any idea what would have happened to you if I hadn't come? Do you have any *clue* about what a foolish, idiotic, dangerous thing it is for you to be doing what you're doing?"

She wanted to bite back at him, but the desolation in his face gave her pause and without wanting to, she felt a definite tug on her heartstrings.

She truly believed that he had her wellbeing in mind. That he was genuinely worried for her.

But that didn't mean she had to do as he said. There wasn't a better or faster way for her to make money.

"I know I was in danger tonight—" she kept her tone deliberately even "—and I am so thankful that you were there, but –"

"Not quick enough," he interrupted.

"What?"

"I wasn't there quick enough, was I?" he spat out in disgust. "I should have walked every step with you instead of waiting by your horse."

He spun away from her and once more, she felt the tension coming off him in waves.

"I can't stop picturing it. His hands on you. His –" He broke off with a muffled oath, and Eleanor stood stock still in shock. She didn't know what to do, what to say.

"I've never felt so murderous in my life," he continued quietly so she had to strain to hear him. "I've never had a cause to."

He swung back around to face her.

"But the thought of someone wanting to hurt even a single hair on your head. Well, you saw what happened."

Eleanor couldn't help it. Try as she might, she could not keep her heart from melting, couldn't quite keep it in her own possession any longer.

And then, he spoke again.

"And now, you tell me that you plan on going *back*?"

He moved closer to her yet again. She was getting dizzy watching him.

"Well, sorry sweetheart, but it's not going to happen."

And just like that, her temper reignited once more.

"No, *I'm* sorry Mr. Grayson." She spoke through clenched teeth. "But you seem to be labouring under a misapprehension that you get any say in this matter. My business is none of yours. And *you* have nothing to do with this."

"Not my business?" He laughed, but there was no humour in the sound. "If you think I'm going to stand by and watch you put yourself in danger time and again, you are very much mistaken, Eleanor."

She was sick of him. He was the one who put her in this position.

The words the fortune teller had spoken to her floated to her mind. *Do not let his past sins colour your view of the future.*

She pushed it ruthlessly away. Along with the voice

that told her he'd tried to make amends.

She didn't want his charity. She didn't want to be an object of pity for him, or a financial noose around his neck.

She would rather risk her life than be that to him.

What he didn't know, what he wouldn't bloody listen to, was that she'd already decided it wasn't safe and therefore would be letting Trevor in on her secret so he could accompany her.

She didn't particularly want her sixteen-year-old brother in a place like that. But she thought the owner liked her and was hoping that for an extra fee, he would allow Trevor to stay in his kitchens or some such place until he was needed to escort Eleanor.

It wasn't ideal. Not by far. But it was better than not earning any money at all.

But here stood this man, the reason for this mess in the first place, attempting to dictate to her as though she were a recalcitrant child.

"I'm going, and you won't stop me," she hissed now, conscious that their voices were rising and so was the risk of someone coming upon them. "I'm in this mess because of you," she shouted, albeit unfairly.

He flinched as though she'd slapped him, but she was past caring.

"I need money. My siblings need money. Trevor wants his commission and, and Pippa deserves the chance to meet someone who will love her and take care of her. And this is the only way I can make that happen."

He was completely silent, studying her intently.

After an age, he spoke. The anger was gone from his tone. Instead he sounded – tender, almost.

"And what of you, Eleanor?" he asked. "What about what you need? What you deserve?"

She opened her mouth but had no response for such a line of questioning.

"I—I—" she stammered and stuttered, wrongfooted by his questions, by the lance of need they sent through her. "When Trevor and Pippa are taken care of, I can worry about me," she mumbled, but the fight was gone out of her.

When Pippa and Trevor were taken care of, it would be far too late for Eleanor to do anything but live here, in this small cottage alone, apart from Mary.

She hated the sting of tears that suddenly sprang to her eyes.

She was tired, that was all. It had been a trying night. It wasn't anything else. It wasn't loneliness or worry for her future.

And it certainly wasn't a craving, a longing for this interfering specimen standing before her.

"You take care of everyone else," he continued, eerily echoing her thoughts from earlier. "Wouldn't it be nice if someone took care of you for once?"

It would be nice. It would be wonderful. But it

wasn't going to happen.

Suddenly, Eleanor felt worn out. Tired in her very bones.

She just wanted to be alone so she could try to get warm. So she could cry her eyes out in peace. So she could spend another night plagued by dreams of this man.

Tristan sighed and it looked as though the fight went out of him, too.

"I just don't want you going back there, putting yourself in harm's way."

"I don't have a choice." The words slipped out before she could stop them.

As Eleanor watched, a sudden blue fire lit his eyes.

"You have one other choice," he muttered, and Eleanor became suddenly wary.

His tone had dropped, become husky and seductive. And it put her on her guard.

She found herself backing up as he stalked toward her.

"Oh?" She meant to sound dismissive, but she sounded merely breathless.

"Indeed." His smile made her toes curl.

"And what's that?"

Surely he could hear her heart slamming against her rib cage.

Surely he could hear the gasping of her breath.

The charming smile became suddenly, utterly wolfish.

"Marry me," he said.

※

Eleanor held her face up to the sun, revelling in the heat on her face, the tangy spray of sea salt on her lips.

She'd been walking the length of this beach for hours and still felt none the calmer.

It was Tristan's fault, of course. As almost everything in her life was right now.

Last night, when he'd rocked her world off its axis with two tiny words, she'd realised that she needed to put distance between them once and for all.

It had been her reaction to his suggestion, a suggestion he hadn't even meant seriously, that did it for her.

For when he'd said, "marry me," her heart had burst with such a feeling of elation her knees had nearly buckled.

She'd realised in that one, unending moment, that she'd stupidly gone and fallen in love with the brute.

And that meant she needed to get rid of him.

For even if his proposal had been sincere, it came from a place of worry. A sense of obligation. Even pity, which she couldn't stand.

After he'd said that last night, Eleanor hadn't been able to move a single muscle, speak a single word.

She'd just stared at him like a simpleton.

And he'd stared right back.

After an age, he had sighed and muttered an oath under his breath.

"I've really made a mess of this, haven't I?" He'd given her a crooked smile that made her stupid heart melt. "You've had a long night. I shouldn't have blurted that out."

Eleanor winced as she remembered the hurt that had stabbed at her. He, himself, was saying he shouldn't have asked. Not two minutes after he'd said it, he had regretted it.

"Go to bed," he'd said softly. "Get some sleep. I'll call on you tomorrow."

And before she could say anything, he'd swept from the room.

Eleanor had locked the door in a sort of daze and made her way upstairs in the same condition.

She'd undressed, donned a cotton nightrail, then lay down in the dark.

And then, she'd sobbed. Great, heaving cries that racked her whole body.

But she was no longer crying because of what had happened to her at the gaming hell.

She was crying because she'd fallen in love for the first time in her life, and had her heart broken. All within minutes of each other.

This morning, when she'd finally made an appearance, Pippa had remarked on how tired she had looked, worried that she was getting sick.

And Eleanor hadn't been sure that she could keep her emotions in check, so she'd left in a hurry, saying she wanted to take a long, *lone* walk on the beach.

Now, here she stood, watching the crashing surf and wondering how in just a few short weeks, her life had become such a colossal, miserable mess.

As she watched the gulls wheel overhead and felt the pleasant breeze loosen the strands of her hair, she had to admit that her life was no more a mess than it had been weeks ago.

If anything, they were far better off because of the money Eleanor was securing every week.

Not once did she worry about getting carried away. Each and every card that was played was counted, each bet carefully thought through. Never had she felt the thrill that her father had constantly chased.

She was only there to win money. To drag her family out of poverty. To give Trevor and Pippa some sort of future.

Yet, she felt so much worse off. Because Tristan Bloody Grayson had awakened something inside her. He'd made her think about herself, about what she wanted. He'd made her long for a life that could never be hers. He'd given her a glimpse of what true happiness could be.

But none of it could be hers.

Because she loved him, whether she wished to or

not.

And he didn't love her.

Being married to him, knowing he had tied himself to her out of obligation or pity, would destroy her.

A lone tear trickled down her cheek, taking Eleanor somewhat by surprise. She didn't think she had any tears left in her.

It was time that she removed Tristan Grayson from her life. It was time to get back to the peace and serenity she'd had before he'd come in and overturned everything. Not that she'd particularly had it, what with her financial woes. But she had a way to combat them now, so once he was out of the picture, her life would be smooth sailing.

Yes. Peace, serenity…

Loneliness, emptiness, boredom…

That inside voice of hers was a pesky little nuisance and nothing more.

"Shut up," she told it, loudly. Like a madwoman.

"I've managed to annoy you before uttering a single word. A new record, perhaps?"

Eleanor whipped round as the voice sounded in her ear.

And there he stood.

Over six feet of pure, solid man.

A man that could potentially be a husband.

But no, that could never be.

She wouldn't allow him to treat marriage to her as a

sacrifice. And she couldn't live with him knowing that he was wishing he were elsewhere.

Most of all, she wouldn't deprive him of a chance to find true love, true happiness.

Usually, Eleanor would have an acerbic remark for him that would bring out his smile that heated her skin and sped up her poor heart.

Not today, though. Today she could only stare at him, knowing she must send him away, wishing she could beg him to stay.

"No pithy comeback from the unconquerable Miss Gold? I feel as though I've won a prize."

Tristan grinned but the expression faded slowly as his eyes ran over her face.

"You look pale." He spoke again, this time all seriousness.

"I'm tired," she said when she finally broke her silence. It was the truth after all. A portion of it.

He reached out and ran a thumb along her cheek.

She shouldn't let him, of course. But she was too weak to tell him not to.

"You're beautiful," he said in response.

This was the time. This was the time to tell him that he needed to walk back out of her life.

That she was happier before she'd met him.

Well, Eleanor conceded, not happier. But oblivious to how unhappy she had been.

Yet she spoke not a word.

And when he bent to capture her mouth in a searing kiss, she forgot all the reasons for wanting him gone.

Instead, she wrapped her arms around his neck, pressed her body to his, and wished with all her heart that he would stay.

Chapter Fourteen

*T*ALK FIRST, KISS *her second.*

All the way over here this morning, Tristan had repeated that very mantra.

It wasn't fair, he knew, to overwhelm her. It wasn't fair to have asked her to marry him after the night she'd had.

It wasn't fair to pull her glorious body closer to his own and delve his tongue inside her mouth before even hearing her answer.

But it would be yes. It had to be yes.

Never had he wanted someone as much as he wanted the green-eyed beauty who'd turned his world upside down.

And not just in his bed, though the mere idea of that added a heat to his desire that he was sure would scorch the earth.

He wanted her in his life. Her temper excited him, her intelligence impressed him, her wit amused him.

Life with her would be filled with arguments, he was sure, since she was the most stubborn, strong-willed woman he'd ever met. But lots of arguing meant lots of making up, and thinking such things made sitting on a horse deuced uncomfortable.

Life would also be fun and safe. They would have a security that neither of them had known as children. For Eleanor would be his equal in every way. Her sharp mind would only help his businesses flourish, and her kind heart would fill their home with more love than he'd ever hoped to have.

He could just imagine a gaggle of blonde hoydens like their mother. He'd be driven demented. And he'd be happier than any other man in the world.

But first, they needed to talk. They needed to really talk. She needed to *listen,* more to the point.

She needed to let him help. Let him take care of her as she had taken care of so many. Let him love her and give her the life she should have. The life he'd taken from her, along with her father.

And so, knowing what was at stake, they would talk first *then* kiss.

That had been his intention.

And then she'd turned and looked at him, and he'd been utterly lost.

It would take a much stronger man than he was to be able to resist the temptation she presented with the sun lighting her hair like a halo, her eyes sparkling like emeralds, her scent surrounding him and captivating him, pulling him closer, weaving him in her spell.

As soon as his lips tasted her own, Tristan felt a

sense of rightness that he'd never felt before.

He could hold her forever, kiss her forever. Just be near her forever. And that's just what he intended to do.

He deepened their kiss, pulling her impossibly close until nothing but the layers of their clothing separated them.

The sound of her moan drove him to distraction.

Somewhere, the last logical part of him knew he needed to slow down. To cool his ardour.

She was an innocent, he was sure.

He knew she considered herself firmly on the shelf, thinking that being slightly older than most debutantes made her undesirable. To Tristan's mind, it just added a maturity and intelligence to her that he'd never seen in the simpering misses whose company he usually kept.

He pulled his lips from hers, trying desperately to regain his control.

But stepping away from her would be an impossibility, and so he trailed a path of kisses down her neck, driving himself a little bit madder with her every whimper, her every moan.

Finally, he lifted his head and looked down at her, flushed with pleasure, pliant in his arms.

She was the most beautiful thing he'd ever seen, and his heart swelled with tenderness.

She pulled his head back down to her own and

much as he wanted to comply, he knew that he needed to take his time with Eleanor, and that they needed to talk.

He knew he needed to be strong.

This time, her lips laid claim on his.

"Please," she whispered against his mouth.

Well, hell. That did it. A man could only withstand so much.

Eleanor was caught in a maelstrom of feeling.

Tristan was a force of nature, consuming every single part of her.

The love she felt for him was overwhelming and made her desire for him all the more potent, all the more difficult to resist.

She felt something shift between them from the moment she'd taken the lead and kissed him, mindlessly pleading with him to give her more pleasure.

It felt as though some last vestige of his control had snapped, and she felt the full force of his desire slam into her.

All she could do was twine her fingers in his hair and hold on desperately as he opened her to a world of lust she had never known herself to be capable of.

His lips once again moved from hers to set a trail of fire along her neck closer, ever closer to the neckline of her gown.

His hands began a slow torturous exploration of her body that set off an ardour she wasn't sure she could withstand.

Suddenly, she felt herself swept off her feet and cradled in his arms before he laid her gently on the sand.

The hot summer sun blazed down on Eleanor's face, and she was momentarily blinded by its glare until Tristan moved over her, gazing at her so tenderly that her heart wrenched.

Before she could come fully back to her senses, however, his lips were once more upon her, kissing her eyelids, touching her mouth briefly before moving to explore every inch of exposed skin.

She relished the weight of him, the evidence of his need for her pressed against her.

"God, I can't control myself around you," he whispered in her ear, before biting the lobe, eliciting a groan from Eleanor.

"Then don't," she cried, hardly able to believe that she was this wanton creature writhing beneath him.

His strangled laugh made him sound as desperate as she felt.

"I must," he answered, his voice strained. "One of us has to keep our wits about us."

He reached a hand up and gently brushed a tendril of hair from her face.

"When we're married—" he smiled, his eyes blazing blue fire "—we won't ever have to stop. We can spend all day, every day just like this."

His words were akin to the cool ocean water washing over Eleanor, and she was shaken from this haze of desire he'd cast over her.

What on earth was she doing?

They were, they were –

Oh, she couldn't even think it without the heat of shame scalding her cheeks.

And it was broad daylight. Anyone could have come upon them.

Then she would have been forced to marry him.

A small, wicked voice awoke in her, *if you were forced to marry him, you could have him without losing your pride.*

It was tempting, especially with her body still alight with the flames he'd stoked inside her.

But nothing had changed.

And she still couldn't believe that he actually meant it.

She wouldn't tie herself to a man who didn't really want her. Or worse, wanted her for reasons that had nothing to do with love.

She had no doubt that he felt lust for her. Perhaps he even liked her. The conversations they'd had, when they weren't fighting that was, had been lively and interesting.

Marriages had been based on a lot less than that, a part of her argued. Most Society marriages had nothing on which to build a relationship. Nothing but a dowry and the correct family name, in most cases.

So why didn't she seize the opportunity while it presented itself?

Tristan was still smiling down at her, looking for all the world like the cat who'd gotten the cream.

He had no idea of the turmoil inside her.

Taking a deep breath, difficult with his considerable weight still on her, Eleanor looked Tristan directly in the eyes, needing to be very clear with what she was about to say.

Needing him to hear it and believe it, for if he were to try to persuade her, she wasn't sure how long she could resist.

"Tristan—" she hated the crack in her voice. Clearing her throat, she tried again. "Tristan, I didn't think you meant it."

It wasn't at all where she'd meant to start, but that's what slipped out.

His eyes widened slightly but instead of looking angry or nonplussed, like she would have expected, he was still smiling.

He rolled off her, and she tried not to miss the weight of him, the scent of him, the feel of him.

Sitting up, he held out a hand to help her do the same.

Instead of releasing her hand when they were both sitting, however, he kept it clasped in his much larger one.

"I knew I shouldn't have said that last night," he began, his gaze fixed on their entwined hands, and despite Eleanor's determination to refuse his offer should it have been sincere in the first place, her stomach twisted with hurt and disappointment.

All the proof she needed that she was only fit for Bedlam, thanks to Tristan Grayson's presence in her life.

Had he changed his mind so soon? Had he been joking from the start?

"Well, no harm done." She tried to sound bright and nonchalant, but her voice sounded brittle even to her own ears. "We can put the whole thing behind us. Now—" She jumped to her feet, righting the bodice that she hadn't even realised had been pulled scandalously low and shaking out her skirts. "I have chores to see to. Good day, Mr. Grayson."

He didn't speak, didn't jump up and try to stop her. He had looked at first confused, and then dazed, but there was no objection forthcoming.

She was glad of it, Eleanor assured herself, as she hurried up the beach and away from him.

It was good that he did not speak or argue. Made the break all the cleaner.

"Eleanor Gold."

His voice boomed across the beach and brought her to a standstill.

She whipped around to ring a peal over his head for shouting at her as though he were scolding a child, only to find that he was standing impossibly close to her.

How had he not made a sound as he'd caught up with her?

"What?" she bit out, sounding petulant, she knew.

He glared at her, looking stunned.

"No harm done?" he finally choked out. "I ask you to marry me, and you want to put the whole thing behind us?"

She didn't know what to say. It would seem that perhaps he had meant it after all.

And that meant that instead of being able to pretend this whole thing hadn't happened and enjoy the memories of the time they'd spent together, they would have to have a conversation she knew would mean she'd never see him again.

Chapter Fifteen

TRISTAN COULDN'T QUITE believe that once again, he'd been tied in knots by this slip of a woman.

He'd damn well nearly taken her virtue there on the beach. He was driven half mad with desire; he'd been tripping over himself trying to find the words to give her the proposal she deserved, and here she stood looking as perfectly put together as though she'd just been freshly pressed and sent outside, instead of coming undone in his arms only moments ago.

Don't think about it, he instructed himself severely. *Don't get bloody well distracted again.*

"I didn't know –"

"So help me, God, Eleanor. If you say you didn't know I was serious one more time…"

"I *didn't* know," she bit back.

She was the most infuriating creature on the planet. He didn't know whether to shake her or kiss her.

Both were preferable.

Tristan took a deep breath, counted to ten – then counted to ten again because the first time didn't do a damned thing for his mood.

He couldn't propose to her whilst he was angry. That wasn't how they should start their lives together.

Besides, she deserved a romantic proposal from someone who wasn't wishing her halfway to perdition.

"Eleanor—" he reached out and cupped her face, forcing her incredible eyes up to meet his. "Sweetheart, would you do me the honour of becoming my wife?"

She couldn't doubt the sincerity in his question. He hoped she could see it in his eyes.

He watched her carefully as she dipped her head and her shoulders heaved on a massive sigh.

Perhaps she was trying not to cry, he thought rather smugly. He had always figured himself the type of man a woman would cry over.

She would cry and say yes, of course, and throw herself into his arms, and then when it was official, they could finish what they'd started on this beach.

He didn't have a ring. He didn't exactly have access to the family vault here in Torrell, Somerset.

Besides, it didn't feel appropriate that he give Eleanor Gold a Grayson family heirloom, not with the way their histories were intertwined.

He would buy something new for her. An emerald perhaps, an homage to her green eyes.

Finally, she looked up and met his gaze.

Her own wasn't tear-filled as he'd expected, and he felt a twist of apprehension in his gut.

Suddenly, he was nervous.

"Eleanor?" he prompted. "Will you marry me?"

Never in his life had he thought he'd propose four times to the same woman.

For a moment, something tender lit her eyes, and an answering tenderness thumped in his heart.

But in moments it was gone and she looked –

Not like Eleanor, his Eleanor. But like the icy, fearsome woman she'd been when they'd first met.

"No," she said, calmly, tonelessly. "I won't."

ELEANOR'S HEART ACHED as she watched the myriad emotions dart across Tristan's face; shock, then hurt, then anger, then rather dangerously, determination.

She had known he wouldn't just accept her answer and move on.

No, he wouldn't leave her alone until she convinced him that it was the last thing she wanted.

It was so unfair that she would have to make him believe she didn't want to be his wife, when it would be the most wonderful thing in the world to her.

If only he loved her, too.

But he didn't. He was a good man. He would do what he could to right the wrongs he'd inflicted on her family, and certainly to try and stop her from ever going to a gaming hell again.

But she couldn't be the reason he was stuck in a

marriage with someone he didn't love.

She wouldn't do that to him.

"You can't be serious," he finally muttered. Only his lips moved; the rest of him seemed struck immobile.

"I am," she said firmly. It was imperative that he see no crack in her armour. "We would not suit. I thank you for the honour, but my answer is no."

She turned again, but she hadn't gotten more than two steps before his hand on her arm swung her back round again.

"Dammit, Eleanor, why are you are acting as though we are strangers? This isn't you."

Eleanor could feel her control slipping. She could feel every single emotion this man had made her feel since they'd first met, no – since he'd won his first hand against her father and changed the course of her life forever, whirling inside her, desperate to get out.

"This *is* me." She tried not to shout, but she was like a woman possessed. She couldn't seem to control what she did or said any longer. "You don't *know* me. You come barrelling into my life after you've *ruined* it and try to order me around."

He looked as though she'd slapped him, and a part of her wanted to take back the words, to throw herself into his arms and spend the rest of her life with him, but her pride wouldn't allow it. And her conscience wouldn't allow him to do it.

"I won't marry you because you're trying to make amends for what you did to us."

"Wait, Eleanor –"

He tried to interrupt, but she ploughed on, determined to say what she had to so she could go home and nurse her broken heart.

"I forgive you, if there is anything to forgive. I appreciate that you tried to help us. But my father was the cause of this, not you. Not really. So please—" The tears that she was desperately trying to keep at bay were beginning to fill her eyes, and she didn't want to cry in front of him. "Please, just leave me alone. I don't want your help. I don't want your pity."

She brushed by him and, again, he wouldn't let her go.

"Eleanor." He quickly moved to block her path. "Listen to me –"

"No," she snapped. "I don't *want* to listen to you. I don't want to marry you. For ten bloody years I've been taking care of this family, keeping our heads above water, undoing the damage that *you* caused."

Eleanor, stop, she told herself, but it was too late. She'd lost all reason. She was lashing out at him with words designed to hurt, designed to make him leave. Words she didn't even mean.

"You made it impossible for me to ever dream of anything beyond keeping us alive with a roof over our heads. And then, when I tried to make things better for

Trevor and Pippa, you interfered in that, too."

"And look what happened to you," he suddenly exploded. "Look what would have happened."

"Are you blaming me for what was done to me?" she screeched, sounding for all the world like a fishwife at a market stall.

"Of course, I'm not blaming you, damn it. I'm just –"

"You're just trying to salve your guilty conscience by marrying me. It will all go away if you give me your name. A house to live in. Money to spend."

"And what's wrong with that?" he shouted. "Why is that so terrible?"

And just like that, Eleanor's anger deflated. The fight went out of her, and she was exhausted—physically, emotionally. She just couldn't do it anymore. She didn't have the energy.

Offering him a sad smile, Eleanor felt the tears begin to run down her cheeks.

"It's not terrible," she said, her tone softer. Because it wasn't terrible. And no doubt, someone far less stubborn than she would have jumped at the opportunity to be his wife.

But what happened to a woman who was an unwanted spouse? She was left alone, that's what. What good were the gowns, the carriages, the houses, and jewels if her husband didn't care for her? If he left her alone whilst he flitted off doing God knew what, because he'd never loved her in the first place?

It had happened to Eleanor's mother. It wouldn't happen to her.

Better to be alone than to be with someone and feel lonely.

"It's very good of you," she continued. "But the fact that you don't understand why I am refusing you is proof that you don't know me at all."

She swept around him and began her walk back to Tide Cottage, her steps slow and sluggish.

"Eleanor," he called, but the fight had gone out of him, too. She could hear it.

She turned back one final time.

"I wish you'd never come here," she said tiredly.

Without waiting to see his reaction, Eleanor turned and walked away.

Chapter Sixteen

"It just seems so quiet without him now."

Eleanor gritted her teeth as Pippa chattered away.

The summer was drawing to a close, and soon it wouldn't be possible for them to sit in the garden like this.

Pippa was sketching, Eleanor was pretending to read, and Trevor was sitting and stewing over something in silence.

She'd given up trying to understand what went on in Trevor's head. She was doing her best, trying her hardest to save enough money for him to purchase a commission, but it wouldn't happen yet.

The truth was that the hell she'd been attending just wasn't making her enough coin to make any real difference to their lives.

At first, compared to the nothing she'd had coming in beforehand, it had seemed like a lot.

And certainly it had improved their quality of life here.

Pippa had made her new gowns, and they'd attended dances at the Assembly Rooms for the first time since they'd lost the manor house.

She had even danced more than once with the magistrate's son and seemed rather taken with the young man, and he her.

Eleanor thought that perhaps by Christmas Pippa would be settled elsewhere, starting a new life, just as Eleanor had wanted.

She had been asked to dance, too, and had even stood up with men she had known as friends her entire life, but had quickly stopped accepting offers.

Rather stupidly, Eleanor found it difficult to dance with another man without thinking of Tristan Bloody Grayson. Even remembering that secret moniker she had for him twisted her heart painfully.

It had been weeks and still the loss of him felt like a great, gaping hole inside her.

After that horrible day on the beach, he'd disappeared, just as she'd wanted.

Eleanor had followed through on her plan and allowed Trevor to accompany her to her weekly games. At first, he'd been furious that she'd gone in his stead, but when they'd talked it through, and she'd explained how well she was doing, he'd grudgingly agreed to accompany her to and from the establishment.

The first time she'd gone after she'd refused Tristan, Eleanor had anxiously scanned the room hoping for a glimpse of him.

But he wasn't there.

And her heart had felt as though it had cracked wide open.

And in the weeks since, despite knowing the outcome would never change, Eleanor anxiously scanned the room, and Tristan still was never there.

"I had thought that perhaps you a-and he—"

Eleanor shook herself free of her imaginings in time to hear Pippa's stilted almost-question.

No doubt her siblings and Mary were more than a little curious about what had made Mr. Grayson just up and disappear one day.

Eleanor never should have allowed him to be in their lives so much. She should have known that people would notice. People would talk.

Why even when she went to the village, she was met with comments and queries about his whereabouts, about what a shame it was that he was gone.

"He and I were friends of sorts." Eleanor worked hard to keep her voice light and nonchalant. Inside her heart was breaking. "Just like you and he were friends. And remember, he was only in Torrell to see to the manor house. P-perhaps he has found a buyer."

"He hasn't." Trevor suddenly spoke up from where he'd been sitting silent as a statue until now.

"How do you know?" Eleanor asked, desperate for any snippet of information, pathetic though it may be.

"Mary was with Cook yesterday, and she told her."

He shrugged but then remained annoyingly silent.

"Well, what did she say specifically?" she finally snapped.

Trevor blinked slowly, uncomprehendingly. "I don't know," he answered.

Eleanor bit her lip to keep from ringing a peal over his head.

It wasn't Trevor's fault that she was up in the boughs about something that wouldn't mean anything to a sixteen-year-old boy.

It wouldn't mean anything to a person who wasn't a madwoman, either.

Just then, Mary came out to hang linens.

"Mary," Pippa called, and Eleanor was delighted her little sister was so inquisitive, for Eleanor's pride would never allow her to question the maid. "What did Cook tell you about the manor house?"

Mary turned and gave Eleanor a knowing look that had her blushing to her roots, but she tipped her chin and tried to look as uninterested as possible.

Mary merely smiled, clearly not a bit fooled, and began pegging linens.

Pippa and Eleanor immediately moved to assist her.

Trevor went back to this stony silence.

"All she said," Mary started without preamble, "Was that the master had come back in a towering rage and informed the staff that he was leaving. Never told them what his plans were, where he was going, when he was coming back. When they asked if they should keep the house ready for his return, he said they should keep it open, close it up, he didn't care. Course, this was all accompanied by language not fit for the ears of young ladies."

Eleanor could just imagine.

"He disappeared to his rooms and not an hour later, he was leaving again. His valet was following him to wherever he was going with his trunks, and that was that."

"How strange," Pippa muttered with a sly glance in Eleanor's direction.

No doubt she was remembering that Eleanor had come home a few weeks past in an equally terrible mood.

"Well, that's no way to treat your servants." Eleanor sniffed piously, hoping that she would sound judgmental enough to fool them into thinking she didn't care. "It sounds like they're far better off without him and his temper around."

"According to Cook, he was a wonderful master." Mary continued hanging her linens. "Kind and courteous and not a bit conceited. In fact, he had been talking as though he were planning on staying in the area. For a goodly while, at least, if not forever. That's what made his sudden departure all the more strange."

She turned then to fix a steely eye on Eleanor, and

once again her cheeks grew unbearably hot.

"Well, well a man is allowed to change his mind, is he not?"

Eleanor knew she sounded defensive, but she couldn't help it.

He'd been planning on staying in the area? That didn't sound like a man who would give her his name to appease his conscience and then dart off to somewhere else.

But that was by the by. It was all over and done with now, and in any case, it still didn't mean he loved her, so it was of little consequence.

Her head knew that. Her heart just needed to catch up was all.

"Of course he is," Mary agreed placidly. "But by all accounts, him changing his mind was unexpected. By Cook's way of thinking, he had been chattering away about readying extra rooms and hiring on more staff. Sounded excited, Cook said, about his future here in Torrell. And then he comes back from a morning walk and – that's it. He's finished with the place, and away he goes."

"Very strange," Pippa piped up again. Most unhelpfully.

Mary bent to pick up her now empty basket.

"Well, something happened to change the poor man's mind," Mary said.

"Poor man?" Eleanor scoffed. "Have you forgotten

that he's the one who landed us here?"

It wasn't fair, she knew, to continue to blame him. Once he'd explained what her father had done, what his *own* father had done, it had been understandable for him to have acted that way.

The moment he'd seen the consequences of his actions, he'd tried to undo them. He'd let go of his hate and thirst for vengeance. He'd let go of the past.

Why couldn't Eleanor do the same? Because, she knew, it was the only thing keeping her from completely falling apart. From hunting him down and begging him to take her back, even if he didn't love her.

She didn't want to be that woman. She wouldn't be.

The truth was she didn't blame him for where she'd ended up, but pretending to was enabling her to get out of bed and face the world every day.

It wasn't Mary, or even Pippa who argued against her.

To Eleanor's surprise, Trevor marched over and stopped in front of her.

"He didn't land us here, Ellie," he said softly. "Father did."

Eleanor's stomach clenched as she gazed up, yes up, at her younger brother.

When had he become so mature? When had he turned from a boy to a young man?

"And Mr. Grayson has done all he can to help us."

She looked from Trevor's sincere gaze, to Pippa's,

to Mary's, detecting a hint of sympathy in their depths, and a lump formed in her throat.

"Well, he's gone now, so what does it matter?" she asked.

None of them answered her, nobody spoke, so she turned and slipped quietly away.

He rather liked Bath. Or he would if he weren't more miserable than he'd ever been in his life.

Tristan downed several fingers of brandy before moving to fill the glass again.

It was, he knew, a little early in the day for being thoroughly foxed.

But nothing seemed to matter to him at the moment. Nothing beyond Eleanor.

And she hated him.

The memory of that day on the beach felt like a kick to the gut.

He could have argued against all her reasons for rejecting him. He knew Eleanor. Knew her damnable pride.

He expected her to point out the disparity in their positions, financial and otherwise. He expected her to insist that she couldn't leave her siblings.

And he was prepared for that.

The disparity wouldn't have existed if it weren't for

her scoundrel of a father. The Gold name had been dulled by that man's behaviours and decisions, but not damaged beyond repair.

Marriage to the son of a viscount, of any Peer, would improve things exponentially for Pippa and Trevor.

He didn't care for money. When Tristan had left to undo his father's damage, he'd made more money than they could spend in a hundred lifetimes.

Trevor would be able to purchase the highest of commissions, Pippa could get as many elaborate Come-Outs as she wanted.

He'd even been readying the manor house for them to move back in, if that's what Eleanor wanted.

If the place held bad memories for her, he'd have burnt it to the ground. Built her a new one, a hundred new ones.

Yes, he had answers for everything.

Everything except the fact that she couldn't really forgive him.

There was no battling something like that, no talking around it.

She could have married him anyway, he supposed, and taken advantage of the opportunity. But she wasn't that type of woman, and thank God for it. Because being without her was hellish enough, but being married to her whilst her resentment grew day by day. *That* would finish him off completely.

So now he was stuck in Bath. Because, idiot that he was, he couldn't stand to be too far away from her. And Bath was only a good day's ride.

Near, yet so far away. A fitting metaphor for their situation.

A couple gentlemen whose acquaintance he'd made whilst staying at the club stopped by for a quick hello and an invitation to join them at a game.

Not the most respectable of places, they informed him, but the winnings tended to be nothing to be sniffed at.

And there was the company of more than one pretty lady.

Tristan kept his smile in place, but his insides twisted in disgust.

He couldn't help but remember that night in the alleyway.

He shook off the memory and bade the gentlemen a swift good-day. He didn't want to go their seedy hell. He didn't want to win their coin.

He wanted the one thing he couldn't have.

He wanted the forgiveness of the woman he loved.

Tristan sat up as he realised that was the first time he'd given voice, even inside his own head, to his feelings.

It wasn't news to him, of course. He'd loved her probably since the first time he'd seen her golden hair spill down her back.

But had he ever actually said the words?

No, he hadn't. He hadn't been given the chance.

He sat back, deflated once more. What difference did it make?

He could tell Eleanor Gold that he loved her more than he ever thought possible. He could tell her that his life was nothing, meant nothing, without her in it.

He could tell her that every single thought he had somehow led him back to her.

But it wouldn't matter.

She had accused him of not knowing her. He knew her too damn well.

His love would mean nothing if he could not also have her forgiveness.

Tristan uttered a black oath and poured himself another drink.

There was no use to any of it. Nothing mattered without her.

Chapter Seventeen

"I CANNOT BELIEVE I let you talk me into this."

Eleanor's hands were shaking, though she was trying her best to keep them still.

Last week she had lost her first game of cards. Lost her first bet.

And it was Tristan's fault.

She couldn't concentrate on anything but him.

Ever since Mary had told her that he'd been planning on making his permanent residence Torrell, she'd had the sickest of feelings that she'd misjudged him.

What if he hadn't proposed out of obligation and guilt?

What if he'd forgotten the past, just as she had, and grown to care for her?

He hadn't said he loved her, but she hadn't said it either.

His actions hadn't been those of a man suffering a sense of obligation. They'd been those of a man who cared for her, and she'd been too blind and stubborn to see it.

And she'd lost him.

Don't let the sins of someone's past colour your view of the future.

It seemed a lifetime ago that the fortune teller had issued those words of advice.

And Eleanor had done just the opposite. Her fear of the past, her fear of loving someone who didn't love her back, had not only coloured her view of the future, but completely ruined it.

She had nobody but herself to blame. That was the kicker.

For Eleanor's whole life she had blamed her wastrel father, her inactive mother, Tristan Bloody Grayson. But this? This was all her fault.

"Don't worry, Ellie," Trevor said beside her now, pulling her from her dark thoughts. "One night at this hell will be like winning ten nights at the other."

Eleanor bit her lip anxiously. She had a funny feeling in the pit of her stomach that tonight wasn't going to be as simple as winning a few hands of cards and relieving silly men of their coin.

"The money we have spent coming to Bath will take a sizeable chunk of whatever I win," she warned, not for the first time.

When Trevor had told Eleanor just what he'd been stewing over, she had been feeling impetuous, heartsore, and restless, so she'd foolishly agreed to come to this hell some friends of his had told him about.

There wasn't much Society in Torrell. But there

was in Bath.

Gentlemen who were rich and played like it. They bet enough to keep the Gold family in luxury for a month.

One night here could change so many things for them.

Pippa had insisted on accompanying them, saying that she and Ellie could shop the day after she'd won them a veritable pot of gold.

Trevor, it seemed, had a big mouth, and had told Pippa just what Eleanor had been doing.

Pippa, being the romantic-minded, fanciful girl she was, thought the whole thing was terribly exciting.

And so the three siblings had waved goodbye to Mary and set off for Bath. They would stay two nights, Eleanor had warned them. And if she didn't win big, they were never coming here again.

"And what will you do by yourself all evening?" she inquired of Pippa. "I don't want to leave you alone at an inn."

Pippa rolled her eyes.

"I will visit with Harriet Smythe," she said. "Just like I told you I would. She moved to Bath when she married last year, and we have kept up a sporadic correspondence. I am quite sure she will be happy to entertain me for the evening."

"And if she has plans?" Eleanor insisted.

"She'll change them," Pippa insisted harder.

It was no use. There was no budging her siblings.

How could she tell them that her heart wasn't in it? That gambling reminded her of Tristan?

Well, she was here now, and that was that.

She would go and win them enough money to make this whole exercise worthwhile.

But after that, she was putting her gambling days behind her. They would find some other way to survive.

HE SHOULD HAVE kept rooms at the club.

Tristan looked at the longcase clock in the corner of the drawing room and sighed.

He was bored. And lonely.

Something he hadn't suffered before he'd gone to Torrell and met the Gold family.

Of course, he was used to the viciousness of the pain he felt in missing Eleanor. But missing all of them was new.

Missing their sharp-tongued maid who had actually warmed to him there in the end. Missing Pippa and her chattering and sewing. Missing Trevor who had also warmed to him and had spoken at length of his dream of donning a red coat and joining His Majesty's army.

He missed the staff at Eleanor's house, which was

how he thought of the place. The cook who had stopped trying to kill him. The butler who had stopped going missing when he needed something.

He even missed the villagers in the sleepy town of Torrell. The ones who knew him by name and greeted him like an old friend, and the ones who were more cautious because their loyalty was to the Gold family.

Tristan would rather be in the tiny but cosy drawing room of Tide Cottage chatting and laughing with the Gold family, Eleanor right there by his side, than be in this cold, oversized, mausoleum of a house that he'd taken.

The sound of someone knocking at the door surprised him.

There weren't many of his acquaintances in Bath at this time of year, or any time really. Certainly none he knew well enough to call on him at such a strange hour.

There were the distinctive sounds of footsteps before a light tap sounded on the study door.

"Enter," he called, standing from the chaise he'd been lounging on.

"A Miss Gold to see you, sir. Alone."

Tristan ignored the obvious censure in the man's tone as his heart burst with pure ecstasy.

Eleanor!

He didn't give a damn that a woman must never call on a man. Not alone. Not at night.

He hoped she wasn't in some sort of trouble, of course. But if she was, it didn't matter, he'd fix it. Nothing mattered save that she was here.

"S-send her in." Tristan heard the croak in his throat, but he didn't give a damn about that, either.

A cloaked, hooded figure stepped through the door then waited while the butler stepped out, giving them a measure of privacy.

Tristan's throat felt dry as an Indian summer as she lifted her hands to the hood of her cloak.

The same heart that had nearly burst from his chest, dropped to his toes with disappointed as the face of Pippa Gold stared back at him.

"Pippa." He tried to keep his countenance, tried not to let his disappointment show. "What are you doing here?"

Pippa eyed him quizzically for a moment before she sighed and shook her head as though she somehow found him wanting.

"I'm here because my sister is utterly miserable. And I want to know what you plan on doing about it."

THIS HAD BEEN a mistake.

Eleanor shuddered as she once again looked round the table at the hostile stares she was receiving.

The men of Bath were far less accommodating than

those in Torrell. Far less tolerant of having a lady of Quality in their midst.

The owner of this particular establishment had been more than a little shocked when Trevor had made discreet enquiries about allowing Eleanor to play.

But the man was a fan of oddities, he'd said, and she'd piqued his curiosity enough to gain entrance.

Trevor had been right, too, about the difference in the money that was lost and won here.

It made her winnings before look like pittance.

When she'd first entered the room, she had stupidly scanned the crowd. Of course, Tristan wouldn't be here, and she'd been annoyed with herself for even contemplating it.

Her first few attempts to play had been met with open hostility and disgust. Nobody would play a woman.

She had been informed in the crudest possible way that women in this place were good for only one thing.

Thankfully, the owner had stepped in, his face stamped with both curiosity and scepticism.

And that, along with the attitude of the clients in the room, was enough to get Eleanor's head into the business of winning.

And win she did.

She ruthlessly pushed every single thought from her head and concentrated on counting the cards, watching her opponents' tells, and calculating the pay-off versus pay-out of each hand.

But as the evening went on, the hostility grew, and Eleanor knew it was time to leave.

She'd just won quite a sizeable pot, and the gentleman who'd lost the most to her stood up so abruptly that his chair had fallen over with a loud clatter, bringing a cessation to conversation and activity around them.

Eleanor felt a snake of fear as all eyes turned to her, and she bowed her head, fiddling with her gloves and refusing to meet the eye of anyone.

When the rumble of conversation started back up she would take her leave subtly and without fuss.

Someone righted the chair, but Eleanor neither knew nor cared who it would be.

The sooner she got out of there the better.

It wasn't worth the pot, Eleanor decided. She didn't feel comfortable here any longer. She didn't want to keep doing this.

"Is this seat taken?"

Eleanor froze.

It couldn't be.

Slowly, Eleanor lifted her gaze.

Fawn breeches, a black immaculately cut jacket, charcoal waistcoat, snowy white cravat.

And that face.

Blazing blue eyes, a stubborn lock of chestnut hair.

Tristan.

Her heart stopped dead in her chest before bursting into a gallop.

"You," she whispered before she could stop herself.

"Me," he smiled.

Without another word, he took the seat across the table and faced her.

Chapter Eighteen

HIS MIND HADN'T done Eleanor Gold justice.
Tristan was finding it hard to breathe just being near her again.

Outwardly he was calm, insouciant, charming.

What she didn't see was that his fists were clenched under the table to keep himself from reaching for her.

How could she expect him to live his life without her? How, when she had become the very centre it?

He watched her cheeks pale, then blush as her eyes, the colour of seafoam in the candlelight, finally met his own.

While he sat, he made sure to keep his eyes locked on her own.

"What are you doing here?" She leaned forward and hissed the question as though she could somehow keep this conversation between the two of them.

They couldn't, of course. All around them, he could hear snippets of gossiping and questioning about what was going on.

Gentlemen, it would seem, could give the biddies of Almack's a run for their money in the scandalous whispering stakes.

"I'm playing cards," he answered smoothly.

Her eyes narrowed suspiciously, and he fought back a grin.

If he played this right, if he won her back, he'd never get anything by her.

And he couldn't wait.

"Well, I'm leaving," she said, albeit shakily.

Tristan watched her closely.

Was Pippa right?

"My sister is stubborn and filled with more pride than is good for a person. She also refuses to see me as anything other than a child to be taken care of. And the same goes with Trevor."

Tristan hadn't known what to say in response to Miss Gold's comments on Eleanor, so he'd stood there like an idiotic mute.

"I don't pretend to know what happened, Mr. Grayson. Eleanor certainly would never say. All I know is that for the first time since we were children, Eleanor looked happy, truly happy when you were with us. And when you left, so did the shine in her eyes and the smile she couldn't quite hide. I am not here to tell you what to do. And I won't speak to you about things that should come from Eleanor. But if you care for her, if you feel what I suspect you feel for her, then you need to tell her. And fast, before it's too late."

She stepped forward and handed him a folded sheet of paper.

"This is where she is tonight. I would hurry, if I were you."

Tristan had been left standing in the middle of the room as Pippa pulled her hood back up then turned and swept away.

His heart had pounded; his mind had raced.

Eleanor was here, in Bath.

But, but she'd rejected him. Four bloody times!

Surely he would be mad to try again?

But it was no use. He'd known the second he found out she was here that he would go to her.

He would propose a fifth time, a sixth, a seventh, a hundredth time, if he thought she would have him.

He had called for his horse immediately and found himself here, sitting across from her, not half an hour later.

Tristan had things he needed to say to Miss Eleanor Gold. And this time, he would make sure she listened to it all.

※

ELEANOR COULD ONLY gape open-mouthed as Tristan leaned back in his seat, looking casual and composed and so handsome it singed her blood just to look at him.

But what was he doing here? In Bath of all places! And sitting at this very table.

It was too much. She couldn't bear it. She couldn't sit across from him and keep her countenance, knowing what she'd lost, knowing what she'd thrown away.

Risking a glance around, Eleanor saw to her dismay that they had garnered the avid attention of almost everyone in the room.

Her cheeks burned hotter still, and she stood, determined to leave before her legs gave out.

"Will you not play a hand against me?" Tristan asked softly, his deep voice running over her, bringing with it a shiver of desire.

This was ridiculous.

"No, I won't," she snapped.

What was he about, in any case? After that day on the beach, surely he'd had enough of her.

Eleanor pushed her chair back and had turned to go when he spoke again.

"Afraid?" he asked casually.

Keep moving, Eleanor Gold. He is trying to bait you.

But when had she ever listened to the voice of reason, who must be exhausted by now?

She turned slowly to face the table once more.

"Pardon me?" she asked and earned a laughing set of "oohs" for her trouble.

It was like a bloody play in here.

"You heard me." He grinned that wicked smile of his that made her toes curl.

"I'm not afraid." She fought to keep her voice steady. "I'm just finished here."

He nodded as though it made perfect sense, then ruined it by opening his big mouth again.

"It does look as though you're running scared. I never thought you were a coward."

She scowled as the crowd laughed and oohed some more. Idiots. Didn't they have anything better to do?

"One hand." He spoke again. "Winner takes all."

Eleanor hesitated.

The truth was she didn't want to walk away from him. She wanted to crawl into his lap and never leave his side.

And she was more than a little curious as to why he'd sought her out. Why he even wanted to speak to her again after what she'd said.

A loud whisper sounded from the crowd that had gathered round the table.

"She won't take the bet. She's a woman, ain't she?"

And that did it.

Without another word, she sat and faced him across the table.

She ignored the audience that had goaded her into this in the first place.

She ignored the fluttering in her stomach as his grin widened and his eyes shone with triumph.

"The stakes?" she asked as calmly as she could.

Tristan studied her for an age, and she wondered what it was he was looking for in her expression.

"One hand," he answered, after eons of her growing tenser by the second.

In her peripheral, Eleanor saw Trevor dart up to the table. He'd taken to sitting in the kitchens, so someone had obviously informed him as to what was taking place.

Gossip really did travel like wild fire.

"Everything you've won tonight," he responded, earning a round of gasps and murmurs from their captive audience.

"Against?" she asked with a raised brow.

Was he trying to bloody bankrupt her?

He knew her skills with cards. But she knew his, too, and they weren't to be sniffed at.

Just what was he up to?

"Everything I brought with me," he answered with a small, secret smile. "Your choice."

DAMN, BUT SHE was good.

Tristan knew her enough to know that she must be facing some inner turmoil, yet outwardly she gave nothing away.

He knew that right now she would be flipping

through everything in her mind, looking at the angles.

She'd never guess what he had up his sleeve though; he was counting on it.

She raised a brow in that way that drove him wild, but he didn't let it show.

Yes, she was good. But so was he.

"You expect me to agree without knowing what you brought?" she asked, sounding amused.

He nodded, watching her the entire time.

The crowd was having a grand old time, but he didn't care. Not once did he break eye contact with the masked woman sitting across from him.

"I do," he answered. "That's the game."

She laughed softly.

"Why would I do that?"

"Makes things more interesting," he answered then waited.

Eleanor wouldn't be rushed, he knew. But he also knew that she was far too stubborn to stand down from a direct challenge, and he was banking on that stubbornness now.

"Come on," he coaxed when she still hadn't spoken. "You know how good you are. I know how good you are. Let's see if you're good enough to beat me."

Her eyes shot green flames at him, and he knew he was riling her. Good. That's what he wanted.

She glanced to the right of his shoulder, but Tristan didn't turn to see who she was looking at. He guessed

Trevor, but he was keeping his eyes on the prize.

She looked back at him, pursed her lips and then finally, mercifully, nodded her consent.

The crowd of an audience clapped and whooped, but it didn't distract Tristan, or Eleanor. She kept her eyes locked on his.

His desire for her was almost painful, but he didn't show it, merely quirked his lips.

She was brave; he'd give her that.

But then, hadn't he known she was brave? She was the most courageous person he'd ever met.

The way she'd taken care of her family, even when she was but a child, the way she'd faced problem after problem, most of them his doing, and risen above every one of them was nothing short of spectacular.

And she had no idea, that was the kicker. She had no idea just how wonderful she truly was.

He eyed the pile of coin and folded notes she'd amassed.

Not to be sniffed at.

He knew the difference a take like that would make to the Golds.

He could only hope she would prefer what he had to offer.

This was the only hand he ever wanted to lose.

Wordlessly, the cards were dealt.

By now, a charged silence had filled the room. No other games were played; no sound was made.

Everyone was watching avidly.

They all thought there was a lot of money at stake.

Only Tristan knew there was a hell of a lot more.

Eleanor lifted her card. Her eyes flicked downwards then straight back up.

She gave nothing away.

She placed the card face down back on the green felt of the table then pushed her sizeable fortune into the middle.

When she was done, she sat back and raised that brow.

Tristan leaned forward.

So did every other person, excepting Eleanor.

It would be amusing if he weren't suddenly nervous as a skittish colt.

He picked up his card, looked, then placed it back down.

And then, he spoke.

"You know—" he kept his tone conversational. "You said once that I didn't know you. That wasn't true."

Under her mask, he saw her frown.

"I know you," he continued. "I know that you love your brother and sister so much that you would do anything for them."

Her eyes darted to his right again, confirming that Trevor stood there.

"I know that you are strong, and brave, and have

faced challenges that would have destroyed another person."

Was that the glint of a tear in her eye?

"I know that you are proud, stubborn, immensely irritating."

She actually growled, and Tristan struggled to keep his face straight.

"Beautiful, intimidatingly intelligent, kind, and courageous."

A tear dripped from under her mask, and he itched to catch it with his thumb.

He never wanted to make her cry again. He hoped these were happy tears.

"I know more about you than you think. After I'd run off to lick my wounds following your countless rejections—" he paused to smile and take the sting out of his words. All around them, people were whispering, no doubt wondering what the hell was going on. "I thought about why you had said no. And something occurred to me."

He paused and waited, though it almost killed him. But he had to make sure she was invested in this, interested in this.

After eons, she huffed out an exasperated breath, and this time he couldn't control his grin.

"What occurred to you?" she asked, her tone tinged with irritation.

"Well, two things really." Tristan was starting to

enjoy himself. "There was no way that your pride would allow you to marry someone if you thought for a second that he was asking because he felt sorry for you, or because he felt guilty about his past behaviour."

Her chin came up a notch, which confirmed Tristan was right.

"And the other thing?" She tried to maintain her façade, but her voice shook as she asked the question and suddenly, he found it desperately hard to speak.

"The other thing," he managed, albeit hoarsely. "The other thing was that I had failed to tell you the reason I wanted to marry you. The real reason. Not that you gave me the chance to."

She smiled a tiny, fleeting smile. But it was enough to give him hope.

Suddenly, a voice piped up from the listening mob. He'd quite forgotten they were there.

"What was the real reason?" it shouted, earning a few chuckles.

"The real reason," he said, only to Eleanor. "Is that I have fallen desperately, insanely, crazily in love with you. And not a minute goes by that I don't wish with all of my heart that you had said yes and become my wife."

Chapter Nineteen

ELEANOR'S WHOLE WORLD tilted alarmingly as Tristan spoke those longed for words.

The horde of people surrounding them went wild. She heard claps, shouts, even a sob or two.

But none of it mattered. Nothing mattered but the man whose gaze hadn't once left her own.

Could she let herself believe this was really happening? That he meant what he said?

She searched the blue depths of his eyes for answers. All she found was tenderness, hope, and – her heart stuttered erratically – and love.

He meant it! He truly meant it.

Eleanor couldn't speak. Couldn't move. He had rendered her completely speechless.

She was so close to getting everything she hadn't even dared dream of, and she couldn't speak a word.

Tristan reached into his pocket and withdrew some folded papers.

He opened them up and, without breaking eye contact with her, placed them in the middle of the table on top of her winnings.

Curiosity got the better of her, and she darted her eyes down.

A quick scan, and she saw immediately what they were.

The deed to their house in Torrell.

She looked back up at him in time to see him reach into his pocket once more.

This time, he withdrew a beautiful emerald ring adorned with tiny clusters of diamonds on either side, placing it on top of the deed.

A wedding ring.

Eleanor wanted to pinch herself to make sure it was real, he was real.

He stared intently at her for a moment then signalled for the next card to be flipped.

The three of hearts.

He looked down at it, then turned his card over and placed it on the table.

The jack of hearts.

All rules of play had gone out the window, but nobody seemed to mind, least of all Eleanor.

She finally dragged her gaze from his to look at his cards.

Wordlessly, she turned her own and placed it face up on the felt.

The queen of hearts.

Her hand beat his. She owned everything in the middle of the table.

Looking back up at him, she saw an unholy fire light his eyes.

He looked – triumphant. That was it.

With a slow, wolfish grin that turned her insides to butter, Tristan sat back in his chair before breaking the agonising silence.

"I win."

THE HELL ERUPTED in a cacophony of sound.

People were shouting, trading money they'd obviously bet between themselves, and slapping each other on the back.

Eleanor and Tristan stayed seated through the entirety of the bizarre celebrations.

She didn't know what to do.

It was so overwhelming. Eleanor, who usually took charge of any and all situations, had been rendered utterly useless.

It seemed Tristan took pity on her for he suddenly moved from his chair and rounded the table.

Kneeling at her side, he took one gloved hand in his own.

"The house is yours, Eleanor," he said softly, for her ears alone. "The ring, too. I had it made here in Bath. I wouldn't keep it, even if you didn't want me. It was made for you."

"Why are you in Bath?"

Eleanor could have kicked herself. After everything that had happened, all the things she wanted to say, and that's what she came out with?

Tristan smiled a self-deprecating smile that melted her heart completely.

"I left when you told me to," he said. "But I found I couldn't bear to be too far away from you."

His eyes bored into her own.

"You're not going to make me ask a sixth time, are you?" he quipped, but she could tell he was nervous. "I mean, I know that wasn't a vocal proposal, but it was a proposal nonetheless."

She opened her mouth to speak, but before she got a chance, he kept going, the words flying from him.

"I don't care if you don't love me, Eleanor. If there was a way for you to forgive me then I don't need more than that. The possibility of you growing to love me is enough for me. But please, don't send me away again. I don't think I can do it. I just want to be with you."

Her eyes were streaming with tears now, Eleanor knew, but she didn't even bother brushing them away.

"I don't need to forgive you," she sobbed, and her heart twisted as his face fell and his head dipped.

She used her free hand to cup his face and bring his gaze back up to hers.

"I don't need to forgive you because I had already forgiven you. I just – I couldn't let you sacrifice yourself. I couldn't let you marry me and give up the chance of real happiness."

"But –" He began to interrupt, but she shook her head to stop him.

"I didn't know you loved me when you asked me, Tristan. And I didn't want you to tie yourself to me. Because—" she blinked furiously at the tears that wouldn't abate. "Because I loved you too much to let you do it. Because I loved you so much, I just wanted you to have a chance at happiness, even if that meant I lost you for good."

His eyes widened at her words, and then the most beautiful smile burst across his face.

As though this whole evening hadn't been scandalous enough, Tristan leaned forward and captured her lips in a kiss that seared her right to her very soul.

Eleanor had no idea how long it went on.

She barely had any idea how she got outside and into the carriage that Tristan had waiting.

She stood in a daze of happiness, of shock, as Tristan sent Trevor back to their inn with the horses then helped her into his carriage.

She thought he meant to sit beside her but was shocked and thrilled when he lifted her and placed her firmly on his lap.

Before his lips descended on her own, however, she pushed him gently away.

"I had the queen of hearts," she said suddenly. "I

won."

"I know that, sweetheart," he said, removing her hand from his solid chest, and placing a kiss on it.

"You said you won." She frowned.

Tristan lifted a hand and brushed a golden tendril from her face.

"You're in my arms, Eleanor," he said softly. "And I'm never letting you out of them again. Of course, I won."

As he kissed her again, making her forget her questions, forget everything except the feel of him pressed against her, Eleanor realised that Tristan was right.

She had won, but so had he.

They would be together forever. They both won.

THE END.

Epilogue

"I'M SO NERVOUS, Ellie."

Eleanor smiled at her younger sister as she helped her adjust her veil.

"It's normal to be nervous, dear. All brides are nervous on their wedding day."

"Were you?"

Eleanor thought back to the day last year when Tristan had placed the intricate emerald ring that he'd had made just for her on her finger.

No, she hadn't been nervous. She'd been eager, frantic even, to start their lives together.

But Tristan and Eleanor had been through so much before they had gotten to that point that their souls were intertwined utterly and completely.

Pippa's courtship with the magistrate's son had been much more traditional and, thankfully, problem-free.

"George is a wonderful man, who loves you," she said in lieu of an answer to that question. "I know he will make you happy."

With the way Pippa's eyes softened at the mention

of her betrothed, Eleanor knew she had nothing to worry about.

Trevor stepped forward, resplendent in his red coat, and held his arm out, ready to escort Pippa up the small church aisle and into her future.

Eleanor looked up from fussing at Pippa's sky-blue gown, and her eyes met her husband's.

As had been the case since their own wedding, everything and everyone around Eleanor fell away until it felt as though she and Tristan were the only people in the world.

Soon, though, even his blue gaze wouldn't be enough to make her feel that way.

Soon their son or daughter would be included in their little bubble.

Nobody knew, apart from Tristan. Tristan, who'd fussed over her like a mother hen from the second she'd told him.

He smiled that secret smile of his that was meant only for her, and her heart stuttered in that now-familiar way.

Never had Eleanor imagined that Tristan Bloody Grayson would make her happier than she'd ever thought possible.

With a cheeky wink, she glided down the aisle past him.

She watched Pippa and George exchange vows, and she could only hope that her little sister would feel even a fraction of the happiness Eleanor felt every day of her life with Tristan at her side.

***

"Alone at last."

Tristan wrapped his arms around his wife, pulling her into his embrace, and felt the familiar stirring of desire that only she had ever been able to elicit.

"It was a beautiful wedding," Eleanor murmured then gasped as his lips found the part of her neck that always drove her mad.

"You were beautiful," he said against her satin skin, revelling in the shiver that ran through her.

"I have an idea," she said breathlessly as his hands moved to undo the inconveniently tiny pearl buttons on the back of her gown.

"Oh? And what's that?"

"Let's play a hand of cards."

Tristan stopped his ministrations and lifted his gaze to clash with her own in the looking glass of their bedchamber.

He saw her breath hitch at his wicked smile.

"The stakes?" he asked, mirroring the question that had finally brought them together.

Eleanor's smile matched his own, causing lust to slam into him.

She turned in his arms and snaked her hands

around his neck.

"Winner gets all," she whispered before she kissed him deeply.

He was already a winner, Tristan knew, as he took control of their kiss. He already had it all.

THE END.

Thank you so much for reading! If you enjoyed this book, please consider leaving a quick review on Amazon. You have no idea how helpful even one sentence can be for me.

Keep turning the pages for a special preview of the next book in the Fortunes of Fate series by author Diana Bold. The Fortunes of Fate series is where 10 Historical Romance Authors came together to loosely knit a series of Regency Happily Ever After's into this delightful Shared World.

Enjoy these whimsical love stories. When fortune and fate collide, love abounds…

Prequel: Fortunes of Fate by authors Christina McKnight and Annabelle Anders

Lord Castleford's Fortunate Folly by author Tabetha Waite

Fortune Favours Miss Gold by author Nadine Millard

Fortune's Gamble by author Diana Bold

Fortune's Wish by author Eileen Richards

Fortune's Dragon by author Meara Platt

A Wallflower's Folly by author Amanda Mariel

Lady Isabella's Splendid Folly by author Sandra Sookoo

The Fate of a Highland Rake by author Tammy Andresen

Miss Fortune's First Kiss by author Annabelle Anders

Fortune's Final Folly by author Christina McKnight

Fortune's Gamble
BY DIANA BOLD

Prologue

June 18, 1815
Waterloo

CHRISTIAN BARNES NEVER meant to assume his half-brother's identity.

But as he stood over Andrew Bradford's lifeless body, the battle still raging around them, the idea entered his brain, making a crazy sort of sense.

Having taken some shrapnel to the leg himself, Christian had been limping toward the hospital tent when he'd seen Andrew fall. Though Christian hated the son of a bitch, he felt no satisfaction in his death. Only an emptiness, a regret for the rift their father had driven between them.

Christian was older by a year, but Andrew had inherited their father's title—Viscount Trowbridge. Christian had entered His Majesty's Service as a mere private, while Andrew had bought his major's commission. Their paths had crossed several times while on the Continent, though they'd never actually spoken. Andrew had made it more than clear that he had no interest in getting to know his father's by-blow.

We could have been twins.

Eerie, really. Like seeing his own death. Both he and Andrew had their father's inky black hair and piercing green eyes, though Andrew's now stared unblinkingly at the smoke-filled sky. So many times, people had confused them or commented upon their likeness. He wondered if Andrew had hated it as much as he had.

A bullet whizzed by his ear, and he started to stumble away, but then his gaze fell upon the epaulettes on Andrew's shoulders, and it occurred to him that he'd get much better accommodations and care as a major than as a corporal. He didn't think his wound was too serious, but he knew how quickly it could turn gangrenous if he didn't get proper treatment.

Before he could think better of it, he'd fallen to his knees at Andrew's side. With a quick glance around to make sure no one was watching, he exchanged Andrew's coat with his own.

Then he knelt there, head bowed, leg throbbing, and stared into his brother's face. With a shudder, he gently closed Andrew's eyes. Could it really be that easy? Could he walk away from this spot as Major Bradford, Viscount Trowbridge?

Quite a gamble. Masquerading as a peer could get

him court-martialed or worse. Were the risks worth the reward?

Pushing himself to his feet, he decided to find out.

Chapter One

LADY REBECCA DAVENPORT made her way through the country fair's maze of stalls and wagons, ignoring those hawking their wares, intent upon finding her cousin Sabrina and convincing her it was time to leave. Since Sabrina spent much of her time in London, she found the Wiltshire fair quaint and exciting, but Rebecca had been here dozens of times, and the appeal of handcrafted buttons and bows had long since waned.

However, before she could catch a glimpse of Sabrina's golden curls, her gaze fell upon something she'd never seen here before. At the fringes of the market, under a copse of trees, sat a small circus. A fanciful gypsy wagon stood to one side, emblazoned with the words *Madame Zeta,* and a gorgeous, exotic woman sat beneath a red tent at a small table in front of it. Her lithe body was draped in a silk dress of shimmering copper, which set off her coffee-colored skin to perfection.

Rebecca found her footsteps slowing, intrigued despite herself. A fortune-teller?

The woman looked up, and her intense light-colored gaze—green or blue?—locked with Rebecca's. A sly smile tilted her full lips, and she crooked a long, elegant finger in Rebecca's direction.

Swallowing, Rebecca moved toward her as though she'd been summoned. As she silently took the chair across the table from the woman, she thought perhaps she *had* been summoned. Perhaps her uncertainty about her future had been evident even across the crowded market.

"Hello," Rebecca said uncertainly, suddenly wondering at her nerve. She hadn't even asked if she could sit down!

Madame Zeta stared at her for a long moment, then gave her a mysterious smile, sprinkling some tea leaves into a porcelain cup and then pouring steaming water over them from an elegant kettle that had sat on a small fire behind her. "Drink," she urged, sliding the cup forward. "We'll see what the leaves have to say."

Rebecca took a sip, surprised to find a smooth Earl Grey, instead of whatever more exotic flavor she'd expected.

"What question do you have for me?" Madame Zeta asked, those bright eyes sparkling with wisdom and knowledge Rebecca would have given anything to possess.

Rebecca blinked, her mind racing. In truth, she had no real answer. Her life had been stagnant for years.

She'd become engaged to Andrew Bradford, Viscount Trowbridge, at her father's insistence, soon after her eighteenth birthday. However, Lord Trowbridge had left with His Majesty's Army soon after, and in the three years since, she'd averaged one letter per year. He seemed to be in no hurry to actually marry her, and so she'd languished at her father's country estate, waiting for him to return.

"Do you see a happy future for me?" she found herself asking, the words surprising her. In truth, she wasn't eager for Andrew's return. Their fathers' lands adjoined, and she'd known Andrew since they were children. Though they'd gotten along well enough, she'd always sensed a cruelty in him, a disturbing lack of emotion. She wanted a home of her own and children, but she wasn't certain if Andrew would treat her well, and she found she wanted to know that even more than she wanted to know when he'd come home.

"Happiness," the fortune teller mused. She stared up at the sky for a moment, as though drawing inspiration from it, then met Rebecca's gaze again, her eyes intense. "I am seldom asked about happiness. Instead, I am asked of marriage and fortune and luck."

Rebecca felt heat race to her cheeks. She took another sip of tea to cover her unease. "I suppose it is a silly question. How does one even measure happiness?"

Madame Zeta shook her head. "I did not say it was a silly question. In fact, I'd say it is incredibly wise. But

I don't need a crystal ball to answer your question, lovely girl. For you see, happiness is a choice. Each day, you can wake up and choose to be happy, no matter your circumstances."

Rebecca laughed, a little disappointed that the fortune teller hadn't been able to give her a glimpse of things to come yet enchanted by her words of wisdom. "You are absolutely right. I will endeavor to do so from now on." She finished her tea and pushed to her feet, fumbling in her reticule in order to offer payment, but the woman reached out and touched her hand, stopping her in her tracks.

"Sit down," Madame Zeta said in a hushed voice. "I feel that there is more I need to impart to you. Let me read the leaves."

Unsettled, Rebecca sank back down in the chair, her gaze drawn to the talisman that hung from a chain around the woman's neck. She pointed at it, intrigued. "What is that?"

The woman smiled and touched the talisman lovingly. "It symbolizes the path of life."

"The path of life?" Rebecca mused, liking the sound of it.

"We are all on a journey," the woman said. "Every twist and turn in the path has meaning." She gazed off into the distance for a moment, then smiled ruefully and drew Rebecca's teacup toward her, staring down at it for a few endless moments.

"Beware the suitor who returns from war," Madame Zeta whispered at last, her voice dropping to a husky rasp that sent a shiver up Rebecca's spine. "He will seem a stranger to you, but he is the one you were meant to find. Look with your heart, not your eyes."

Rebecca swallowed, disturbed at the way the fortune-teller's tone had changed. When Rebecca had sat down, the woman had seemed at ease, amused even. But now it seemed as though she actually had seen or felt something. Her words were very cryptic, and Rebecca had no idea what to make of them. The advice of choosing her own happiness had made far more sense to her. Perhaps that was what she'd been meant to hear today, and she tried to shake away the feeling that some actual magic had been at work here.

Madame Zeta blinked and gave her a rueful smile. "Stay here for just a moment longer. I have something for you." She pushed gracefully to her feet and opened the back of her wagon, revealing a glimpse of colorful fabrics and gleaming wood. She opened one of the many cupboards and picked through some items in a small bowl.

Rebecca glanced away, looking through her reticule once more, placing a few shillings on the table. When she glanced up, Madame Zeta had returned. Her gaze seemed to pierce through Rebecca's soul as she pressed a small talisman into her palm. Rebecca looked down, unsettled. It was the size of a coin, with something resembling the Roman number two etched into it.

"What's this?" Rebecca asked, wondering if she really wanted to know.

"Gemini. It represents duality. The twins. Perhaps it will help you to see both sides of the issue."

"What issue?" Rebecca whispered.

"The one you are soon to face, my child."

The talisman seemed too expensive and old to just be given to her, but Madame Zeta shook her head when Rebecca tried to give it back.

"Keep it," the gypsy whispered, a deep sadness in those striking eyes. "I hope you find the happiness you seek."

Rebecca nodded and turned swiftly away, chiding herself for having been so foolish in the first place. A fortune-teller? She wasn't a child to be taken in by such silliness. Still, the woman's words were ones to ponder. Perhaps she had been simply drifting along, waiting for her life to start for far too long. She needed to stop looking to the future and start living for today.

"What did you buy, Becca?" Sabrina asked, coming up alongside her and jarring her out of her thoughts.

Rebecca glanced down at the talisman again, then clenched her fist around it, shoving it into her reticule. "It's nothing. Just something the gypsy gave me."

"A gypsy!" Sabrina cried, looking around with excitement. "I want to talk to the gypsy!"

Rebecca shook her head, pulling her along. "I've a

bit of a megrim, and we've been here far too long already. May we head home? Please."

Sabrina's pretty face fell, but she nodded her blond head. "Of course, dear. Let's go home."

They headed back toward their waiting carriage, but right before they reached it, Rebecca glimpsed a sight that made her blood run cold, especially given the conversation she'd just had with the gypsy woman. A man rode down the lane toward Trowbridge Manor, the sun glinting off his black hair, his large body moving gracefully on his fine mount.

He was too far away to call out to, but she'd recognize him anywhere.

Her fiancé had returned.

About Nadine Millard

Nadine Millard is a bestselling writer hailing from Dublin, Ireland.

When she's not writing historical romance, she's managing her chaotic household of three children, a husband and a very spoiled dog!

She's a big fan of coffee and wine with a good book and will often be found at her laptop at 2am when a book idea strikes.

Connect with Nadine!
Website: nadinemillard.com
Newsletter: eepurl.com/dNCiX-
BookBub: bookbub.com/authors/nadine-millard
Amazon: amazon.com/Nadine-Millard/e/B00JA9OXFK
Facebook: facebook.com/nadinemillardauthor

More Books by Nadine

The Saints & Sinners Series
The Monster of Montvale Hall
The Angel of Avondale Abbey

The Ranford Series
An Unlikely Duchess
Seeking Scandal
Mysterious Miss Channing

The Revenge Series
Highway Revenge
The Spy's Revenge
The Captain's Revenge

Standalone Romances
Beauty and the Duke
The Hidden Prince

Made in the USA
Middletown, DE
04 May 2019